CW01498921

Conversion - A Transgender Tragedy

Copyright 2019 Debbie Ballard

1st Edition - 2019

Although this project is based on a great deal of personal experience and years of research, including online and local support groups for the LGBT community, this work is fictitious, and any similarities to any persons, alive or dead, are purely coincidental. Mention is made of persons in public life only for the purposes of realism, and for that reason alone. Certain license is taken in respect of medical procedures, terms and condition, and the author does not claim to be the fount of all knowledge.
The author accepts the right of the individual to hold his/her/their own political, religious, and social views, and there is no intention to deliberately offend anyone. If you wish to take offense, that is your choice, but it is not my prime intent. This book IS intended to provide insights into the fears, concerns, and courage that members of the LGBT community must experience in order to be who they are and experience love.

Preface

This book is dedicated to the memory of two of my cousins, Mark Woodworth, and David Lundberg, both of whom ended their lives at a very young age. David was 11, Mark was 14. I knew from personal experience that they were transgender and/or gay. However, this story is fictional, but well researched.

This book covers many forms of "conversion therapy", some of which are still widely used today by religious organizations.

My own mother had many of the treatments described, and others I had learned about when I tried to discuss my own desire to be a girl at age 8 and 9. My father told me on his deathbed what would have happened if I had not kept silent about my own transsexual identity. This was also when he told me, "Be yourself, even if that means being Debbie!"

This is not a pretty story, not a happy love story, and I have done my best to limit sexual events necessary to the plot to brief references. In addition, many of the techniques described in the treatment are no longer used, they are considered unethical, but are used by some religious fanatics who engage in Conversion therapy.

Table of Contents

Horrible Discovery:

Lois knocked on the door for several minutes but got no answer. Finally, she opened the door.

"Mark, dinner is ready, I've called you down several times, and knocked for several minutes, why didn't you answer? Get up sleepy-head!"

Lois reached to Mark and tried to jostle him, but he wasn't responding. She pulled on his shoulder. Still no response. Something was wrong.

"Mark, you need to get up now, you've been sleeping way too long. Time to get up."

She pulled the covers off, shocked to see him wearing a blouse and a skirt. But worse, Mark wasn't responding. Then she felt his head, it was warm. She reached to feel his neck, but she couldn't find a pulse! Then she found it, his heart was barely beating.

"Lloyd! Something is wrong with Mark, call 911! We need an ambulance, NOW!"

Lloyd walked up the stairs, into the room, and saw the outfit. "I'll call 911. Get him out of those ridiculous clothes!"

Lois stripped the body, leaving him naked, then slipped on a pair of jockey shorts. Then she felt his pulse again. She found nothing. She broke down completely, "Oh MY GOD NO! Lloyd, I think MARK is DEAD!!!"

Lori walked in to hold her mom. She noticed that the bottle of pills next to the bed was almost empty and saw the pint of brandy on the floor. "Mom, I think he killed himself! His pills are gone, and there was a half a bottle there last night. Look at the bottle on the

floor. He's not supposed to drink on his lithium and the sedatives, booze, and lithium are a deadly mix. We have to get out of this room NOW mom. The police will need to investigate. Whatever you do, don't touch ANYTHING!"

Lois was in shock, "He was dressed as a girl again, so your dad made me strip him. I'll just cover him up again."

Lori shook her head, "No, Mom, you can't touch ANYTHING! Even stripping him could make the police suspicious. Let the police handle it."

Minutes later, the ambulance arrived. It was too late, Mark was gone. A few minutes later, the police arrived and sealed off the room. Two detectives arrived and started to look around.

Detective Lou Harris looked at the body and everything surrounding it. Immediately, things looked wrong. "John, how many 14-year-old boys fall asleep in a cold room with no blankets, pajamas, or clothes?"

Lou looked at the pills, "This prescription is only two weeks old, there should be at least 20 pills, but there are only 5. The brandy bottle is open, almost empty. Lithium in the prescription bottle, not getting high. It looks like this might be a suicide attempt."

John nodded, "Yes, but we need to examine the scene. Look here, where the underwear is riding up. There is a crease, like he was wearing something tighter, and a bra line. The clothes were changed. The scene has been disturbed. Let's take a closer look, shall we?"

They opened the drawers of the dresser. The bottom drawer front was nearly a foot deep, but John noticed that the bottom seemed to be only 6 inches. "Interesting, let's see what you were hiding, some drugs maybe?"

Conversion

John found a small hole just big enough for his little finger and pulled on the bottom. It came up. What he saw stunned him. "I think we need to investigate further, he may have been bullied."

True Self

It had been a warm summer day. Mark was only 6 years old, and his mother was taking a nap with his new baby sister Linda. She was so tired. He ran into the house crying, followed by his 9-year-old brother Steve.

Steve tried barged into the shared bedroom, "Mark, you're such a sissy! We were just having fun with you, and you started crying like a little girl. Maybe you should play with Lori instead!"

Mark snapped back, "Yeah, I should! I have a LOT more fun with HER than I do with you and your bully friends. I don't want to play football, I don't want to wrestle, and I don't want to fight! Just leave me alone!!"

Steve was fed up. "Fine, go play with the GIRLS. You know how much dad hates that. He'll probably take the belt to you when he gets home but have fun with your little GIRL friends!" And stormed out.

Mark went outside and went to the house next door. He rang the doorbell and was greeted by Mrs. Smith.

"Hello Mark, Lily is upstairs, would you like to go upstairs and join her?"

Mark was so polite, "Yes, thank you Ma'am, with your permission of course, thank you."

Peg Smith was always delighted by Mark's manners, so much nicer than his older brother.

"Go right on up Mark, I'm sure she will be glad you came"

Mark went up to Lily's room. Even though the door was open, he knocked on the door.

Conversion

Lily looked up and was immediately delighted, "Marcia! I'm so glad you're here, I'm so happy to see you!"

Mark smiled, "Hi Lily, I couldn't stand Steve and his buddies another minute. Boys are so mean!"

Lily nodded, "I saw from my window. Even Jerry's little brother was picking on you. They kept beating you up. I am so glad you're here instead. Come on, we can play with my baby dolls and my Barbie Dolls."

Mark went to his favorite doll, a baby doll with soft skin, and put the bottle in its mouth.

"Here Linda, I'll feed you. You are such a good little baby! I love you."

Lily picked up the other doll, a larger one, and pretended to feed her with a spoon.

"How come you call your baby Linda, like your baby sister?"

Mark smiled, "I like my baby sister. She's so cute! Sometimes I get the diapers for mommy and hold the safety pins for her. Then mommy lets me hold her for a while. She even smiles at me. It's fun having a real baby, but mom doesn't let me play with her very much."

Lily smiled, "Well, a real baby isn't a toy, and they are more easily hurt than our dolls."

Mark smiled, "Yes, Mommy has to hold Linda all the time, and when Linda falls asleep, mommy sleeps too. She wanted Linda so bad."

Conversion

Lily nodded, "Real babies are a lot of work. My mom takes care of my little brother Georgie all the time and he's almost 2 years old. Mom didn't let me hold him, because I was too small."

After about an hour of playing house and playing with the baby dolls, Lily smiled.

"I got some new outfits for my Barbies; did you want to do a fashion show?"

Mark smiled and carefully tucked his baby Linda doll into the toy crib. "Yes please, I'd love to".

Lily pulled out two Barbie dolls and a little case full of outfits. "Pick out an outfit for your Barbie".

Mark picked through the clothes. He found a cute miniskirt and a flower power tunic, then a pair of white go-go boots. He quickly dressed his Barbie in the outfit he put together.

Lily's eyes widened, "Marcia, that is SO CUTE!! It's too bad you're a boy, you would be a really pretty girl. You really seem to know how to put together really cute outfits! I love it!"

Lily finished dressing her Barbie in the new outfit. "See, my mom got this for me for my birthday!"

Mark pulled out a red hat and put it on the Barbie. "The hat brightens the dark blouse and skirt. It needed some color!"

Lily giggled. "You're right, that looks much better!"

After a few more outfit changes, they decided to color. Lily gave Mark a coloring book.

Conversion

Mark would ask Lily for the crayons he wanted. "Could I have a teal and a turquoise please?"

Lily giggled, "which one is teal?"

Mark smiled, "Teal is a light blue-green, that one there." He pointed to a crayon tip.

Lily pulled out the crayon and read it. "You're right, it's teal. At school, most boys only see red, yellow, green, blue, purple, black, and white."

Mark smiled,, "I see lots of different colors. I have a box of 64 crayons at home. I want the box of 128 colors for Christmas."

Lily colored her picture, and it was a bit flat, but she was happy because she had stayed in the lines. Then she looked over at Mark's picture, it was different., "Wow, Marcia, your picture looks almost alive"

Mark smiled. I like to blend the colors together to make it look more like there is light on it. That's why I need more colors, to bring out the shiny parts and the shadows.

Lily put on a record, a kid's song was playing. Mark and Lily sang together. Mark was on pitch and helped Lily find the right pitch. They also did a little dance that went with the song.

Mark heard a bell,, "That's my mom, ringing for me to go home. Thank you, Lily, I have so much fun playing with you!"

Lily smiled, "I like playing with you too Marcia, I don't know why you even try to play with those nasty boys as Mark, they are so mean to you!"

Conversion

Mark looked so sad, "I don't want to, but my dad says I have to. He doesn't want me to be a sissy."

Lily giggled, "I wish you were my sister!"

Mark nodded, "I wish I was too! Every day! Lori is only a year younger, maybe she can play with us too sometime."

Mark went back to his own house. His mom met him at the door. "Hi Mark, you need to get washed up, your dad will be home in a few minutes, and then we'll eat."

Mark nodded, "Yes Mom, I'll get washed up and help you get things ready."

When he came back down, Steve was watching baseball on TV. Mark went into the kitchen. "All clean, what can I do to help?"

Lois smiled, as Mark showed the front and back of his hands, which were clean. "Could you set the table?"

Mark was cheerful, "Of course Mom, I'll do it right away!"

Lois smiled, Steve never seemed to help, saying it was "women's work", but Mark was always happy to help any way he could. He didn't care that his father thought it was "women's work".

Lois handed him a pair of pot-holders and pointed to a small pot. "Could you please take the peas to the table?"

Mark smiled and took the bowl of steaming hot peas to the table. He put it on the trivet to the left of center. He came back to get the corn, which he placed to the right of center, closer to the head of the table. "Did you want me to take out the potatoes?"

Conversion

Lois smiled, Mark was so eager to help, "No honey, that's a bit too heavy for you to carry."

Lloyd walked in just as Lois was bringing out the potatoes. "I'm home!" and walked into the living room.

Lloyd sat in the recliner, "Steve, how's the game going?"

Steve smiled, "The Cardinals are ahead by 4, 5th inning."

Mark came out, "Dinner's ready daddy, and I helped!"

Lloyd was stone-faced, "Doing a bunch of Women's Work again, Mark? Do I have to put you in a dress?"

Mark smiled, "I just like to help mommy."

Lloyd shook his head, "You should be watching baseball with Steve. Football season is starting soon, we need to get you registered for Peewee league."

Mark started to whine. "I don't want to play football, I just get beat up."

Lloyd shook his head, "No, you have to play football, it will toughen you up. Maybe after dinner, we can play catch in the yard."

Mark was silent, he didn't want to play catch.

Throughout dinner, Mark was silent. They had said the family prayer before dinner, and Mark hadn't said a word.

Stevie regaled Lloyd with tales of his victories in a neighborhood touch football game in the park. Then Stevie said, "Mark was such a baby, he got hurt and ran home."

Conversion

Lloyd stopped eating, "So, Mark, where did you run off to? Not that Lily girl's place again!"

Mark looked down at his plate, finishing the last of his peas. He didn't want to answer, so he pretended not to hear.

Stevie was gleeful, "I saw him coming out of her house when mom rang the bell. I guess he'd rather play with GIRLS than play with us guys. He's such a sissy!"

Mark was mad now, "At least Lily doesn't act mean to me and beat me up! They dog-piled me!" He started to cry.

Lloyd was angry, "Do I need to get the belt?"

Lois snapped, "He's playing with a girl his own age, and he likes her. You don't need the belt."

Lori still hadn't eaten her peas, she was just pushing them around the plate.

Lloyd huffed, "Lori, no desert unless you eat all your peas."

Mark turned to Lori. "Lori, mix the peas with the mashed potatoes, it will taste good! Do you want me to help?" Lori nodded and smiled.

Mark got a spoon full of mashed potatoes, mixed them with the peas, and added a little butter. "Try it now Lori"

Lori took a bite and smiled. She finished the potatoes quickly. "Thanks Markie, you good cook, like Mommy"

Lois brought out ice-cream and pancake syrup. Everybody liked the easy desert and finished quickly.

Conversion

Lloyd pushed away from the table, "Great dinner honey, I need to work it off, boys, let's go play catch."

Mark stopped short. "I'll help mom with the dishes. She did all the cooking, I can help clean up."

Lloyd growled, "That's Women's work. You're not a girl, you're not going to be a sissy, now get out there and play catch."

Mark went out to the yard like he was walking to his execution. Lloyd passed the ball to Steve, a gentle loft. Steve fired a bullet pass at Mark's head. The ball hit Mark's glasses. Mark started to cry.

Lloyd was so annoyed, "Mark, you're just a damn sissy. Go inside; Steve and I can play catch without you."

Mark ran into the house while he had the chance. As soon as he got inside, he stopped crying, and went into the kitchen. "Dad said I could help you after all. He wants to play catch with Steve."

Mark told Lori to pick up the spoons and forks, so she didn't hurt herself on a knife, then he cleared and stacked the plates, and brought them in to his mother. Then he went back and picked up the knives and glasses.

Lois smiled, "Thank you Mark, you do such a good job helping, and you're teaching your little sister to help too. Good for you! Thank you so much. I love you!"

Mark beamed with happiness, "I love you too mom."

Mark went up to his room and pulled out a book. It was a Nancy Drew mystery. Even though he was only in 1st grade, he had taught himself to read, and quickly read as many books as he could. Lois had taken him to the library, and he had asked if there was a book

about a brave girl, and the librarian took him to the Nancy Drew mysteries. Mark enjoyed the book. He had already figured out who did it but was curious how long it would take for Nancy to find out, and what kind of trap she would spring before she did.

When Lloyd came up to Mark's room, Mark hid the book. "Time for bed Mark, no bath tonight, but you should wash your face and hands."

Mark smiled, "I already washed my face and hands daddy. I'm ready for bed. Tuck me in?"

Came over to the bed and lifted up the covers, and the book dropped out of the blanket.

He picked up the book. "Nancy Drew! Why are you reading this sissy stuff? You should read good books! Have you read any stories from your children's bible?"

Mark smiled. "Yes, it's right here", tapping the book by the table, "I've read all the stories."

Lloyd didn't believe it. "Which was your favorite?"

Mark smiled. "Daniel in the lion's den, David and Goliath, and Esther".

Lloyd was stunned. "Esther?"

Mark smiled. "Yes, she was taken to live with king as his wife, and she asked the Eunuch to help her make the king fall in love with her. She won the king's heart and saved all of the Jews from being wiped out.

Lloyd smiled. "I had forgotten that one. I don't think your grandpa ever read me that story. Sounds interesting."

Conversion

Lloyd tucked Mark in and have him a good-night kiss. "I love you Mark, I just wish you were more like your brother."

Mark smiled. "Stevie is like Goliath, I'm more like David, or Esther."

Lloyd shook his head. "Maybe like David, but not like Esther, she was a GIRL."

Mark snuggled and fell asleep quickly.

Awakening

Mark got home from school early. It had been a half-day at school, the last day of school. He had walked home with Lily and the rest of the girls. The boys taunted him the first block or so, calling out "Sissy" and "Girlie-Boy", but Mark had just ignored them. He had long since given up being one of the guys and avoided them as much as he could.

When they got to Lily's house, they went up to Lily's room. Lily opened her closet, and the other three girls started looking at the clothes.

Sarah, a brunette held up a red top. "Can I try this?" Lily nodded.

Mark smiled. "That really brings out the auburn in your hair, and your green eyes.

Helen, a blonde pulled out a dress. "This is a pretty blue dress; can I try it?" Lily nodded.

Mark smiled, "The turquoise color brings out your blue eyes, and your blond hair, it also gives you more color. It almost looks like you're blushing. Thinking of some boy?" They all giggled.

Judy, a redhead with freckles asked Mark, "What would look good on me?"

Mark went to the closet and pulled out a mini-dress "This aqua brings out your hair color and looks good with your complexion, you have such cute freckles. You'll look like an Irish Ginger."

The girls started getting dressed right in front of Mark. They didn't seem to care that he could see them, and he didn't stare or make comments. He helped them get dressed and zipped up the dresses.

Conversion

When everybody was dressed, they looked at each other, they all smiled. "Mark, you were right with all of these, they look great on us. Too bad you have to wear boys' clothes."

Mark nodded. "Yeah, boy's clothes are so BORING. No color, no shape and not comfortable either. It took the whole year to grow into these jeans. This flannel shirt itches, especially now that it's almost summer. Thank goodness I'll be able to wear shorts soon. Even those will be blue or black. BORING!"

Lily smiled, "It seems a shame that all of us look so pretty and you are stuck in those BORING ugly boy clothes. If you could wear something, what would you pick?"

Mark went to the closet. He pulled out a lavender top and a cayenne skirt. "The lavender in the top would bring out my freckles and would go with my light brown hair. The cayenne skirt is such a vivid red that it would give me a pop of color. Not BORING!" They all giggled.

Lily gleamed. "I LOVE it! You absolutely HAVE to try it on. I want to see you in it! Right girls?"

The other girls joined in, "Yes, you'd look wonderful, put it on!"

Mark was scared. "If the boys found out, they'd beat me to a pulp. My dad would have a fit, I might even get the belt... but it is really cute!"

Sarah whined, "Oh, PLEASE!! There's no more school, so you don't have to play with those horrid boys anymore, and it's just this once in the house. Nobody but us has to know."

Mark didn't want to disappoint his friends. "It is a pretty dress, and I do feel out of place. OK, I'll try it!"

Conversion

Lily went to her drawer she pulled out a pair of tricot panties from the package. "You have to wear girl's underwear too. I don't want you wearing ugly boy underwear under my pretty clothes."

Mark nodded, "OK, but I'll put these on, and the skirt, in the bathroom. I don't want you guys seeing me naked." The girls grinned, "OK, but you HAVE to model the outfit once you're dressed."

Mark took the whole outfit into the bathroom with him to get dressed. At least he didn't have to zip up the top. He stripped all the way down and got completely dressed. He was surprised at how comfortable he was. He was so small that he was flat down there.

He dressed in the clothes and looked in the mirror. He wanted to cry. He looked so pretty in this outfit, but with no hair on his head, he looked wrong. "I look terrible."

"Mark Woodward, you get out here right now. You promised and we want to see you." Lily barked.

Mark walked out, feeling like an idiot. He liked the pretty clothes, but he was so obviously a boy in a dress. "My dad gives me buzz cuts every month. I hate it, and I look terrible. I wish I could grow my hair long like you."

Lily smiled. "I'll be right back."

She came back with a wig almost exactly the same color as Mark's hair, what little he had of it.

Lily brushed it out. "My mom got this when she got a perm she hated, but it's relaxed now, so she never wears this. Let's see what you would look like as a girl!" She put the wig on Mark's head and brushed it out. She stepped back and all eyes widened.

Conversion

Mark was about to cry. "Is it that terrible? I'm sorry, maybe this was a really bad idea. I'll change back."

Lily stopped him. "No Marcia, you look better than any of us. You are a beautiful girl. Look in this full-length mirror. What do you see?"

Mark was stunned. He smiled and the girl in the mirror smiled back. Her high cheekbones, cute freckles, full lips, big beautiful eyes, and long hairless legs looked so feminine. She had long slender legs with nice knees. He was just stunned.

All the girls were awestruck and quickly started telling him how pretty he was. Lily went into the bathroom and took his clothes and locked them into her footlocker. "You get to be Marcia for the rest of the day."

Mark started to panic. "What if I get caught? What if my dad or brother find out? What if someone else finds out. I will get the belt for sure! I should change back."

Judy and Helen begged, "Please stay as a girl and play with us girls! You look so good! You are so pretty! You KNOW you have ALWAYS been one of the girls as far as we're concerned, so why not ENJOY being a girl for a while."

Mark began to relax. "OK, I guess it will be OK, but when my mom rings the bell, I'll have to change back."

They spent the rest of the afternoon singing and dancing to records, talking about their favorite bands, and boys. Then they got to Mark.

Sarah grinned. "So, Marcia, which guys or girls do you like? Any of us a love interest?"

Conversion

Mark smiled. "You guys are all my friends, but I don't dream of kissing you or anything."

Judy grabbed his knee. "Are you boy crazy? Who is it?"

Mark giggled, "Stop! OK!" He caught his breath. "Dean Jones, and Davey Jones of the Monkees. I dream of kissing them."

Helen smiled. "How cool, you really ARE a girl! Any guys at school that you think are cute?"

Mark shook his head. "No! Most of them have been mean to me all year long. Hard to fall in love with a bully."

Sarah started to tease him. "Did those nasty boys make fun of you? Poor baby!"

Helen glared at Sarah. "Sarah, didn't you ever look at the boys playing in the field during lunch or gym? They tripped him and kicked him until the bell rang. It must have hurt like hell."

Mark winced at the last word. "Hell is eternal torment, according to Pastor Jim. The kicking really did hurt, but it did last 20-30 minutes. I'd have to curl into a little ball so I could protect my face and stomach. They did break a rib once. I've been in the hospital a couple times."

Helen giggled. "Mark is our spy in boy-world."

They all started to giggle and sing, "Secret Agent Man".

They heard the bell ring.

Mark looked so sad as Lily got his clothes. "I had so much fun with you girls today; I wish I didn't have to go back to being a boy."

Lily smiled. "Who says you have to quit? You can be Marcia any time you come to my house!"

Mark went to the bathroom and started to change back. He got down to the panties and asked, "What do you want me to do with the panties?"

Lily answered from outside the door. "Wear them home. You can put them on before you come over next time. I can't wear them now, and I can't give you a new pair each time you want to be Marcia."

Mark pulled his jockey shorts over the panties and pulled on his baggy jeans. He pulled on his shirt. As he came out of the bathroom, he looked so sad. He handed the wig to Lily. The girls all gave him a good-bye hug, and he walked back to his home.

When he got home, Lois said, "Go wash up and you can help me with dinner."

Mark went to his bedroom, and pulled off his pants, shorts, and panties, which he put in the back of his underwear drawer. He got redressed and washed his hands.

Lois smiled, "I'll let you make the spaghetti. You need to brown the meat and start the noodles. I'll chop some vegetables for the salad. At least we don't need potatoes today.

Mark had become quite good at cooking, and Lois was happy to have the help. She was thinking about going back to work now that Linda was older. Still, she dreaded having to work AND having to do all that housework.

Mark put on an apron and started cooking. Lois watched as she chopped the vegetables, but it was clear that Mark knew what he

was doing. Mark seemed to have a talent for cooking. He browned the meat, added the tomato paste, and added some seasonings. The Italian seasonings were standard, but then he added a teaspoon of brown sugar and a dash of cinnamon.

Even from across the kitchen, Lois could tell that this was going to taste wonderful. Mark seasoned by smell, only tasting when he thought he had reached the final result. He went to the fridge and added a dash of Worcestershire sauce. The scent was magical, and Lois couldn't wait to try it. She went over to the stove, and Mark kissed her cheek. "You can taste it when I serve it."

Lois helped Mark set the table as the sauce simmered, and the noodle water boiled. They had finished setting the table and waited for the sound of the car door. As usual, Steve was watching TV. At least this time he was watching a kid's show with Lori instead of the sports he usually watched.

They heard the car door shut, Lloyd would be inside in about 30 seconds. Just long enough to add the noodles. Mark was taking off his apron as Lloyd walked through the door.

Lloyd had given up hope on turning Mark into a jock. Mark was getting straight A's in school and was reading at high school level. He had an IQ of over 160. Why he insisted on doing "Women's work" Lloyd didn't understand, but he had stopped caring.

Lois called out, "Dinner will be ready in about 15 minutes. You can watch TV with the kids while we finish up."

By the time Mark plated the food, everybody's mouth was watering. As they started eating Steve couldn't help himself. "Mark, you may be a sissy, but you're a better cook than Mom!"

Lloyd rolled his eyes. "Yes Mark, you'll make some lucky lady doctor a wonderful wife someday."

Lois looked over at Mark expecting him to be upset, instead he had a serene happy smile on his face. Something was different. Pride in work well done perhaps? "You have done a wonderful job Mark, thank you."

Linda didn't want to eat her string beans. She looked over to Mark. "Markie, fix beans please?"

Mark went to the refrigerator and pulled out some mustard and some Miracle Whip. He cut up the beans into tiny pieces and added the other ingredients. Linda took a taste and immediately finished the rest of the beans on her plate. "More please".

Lois was astonished, Mark had figured out ways to make both Linda and Lori like their vegetables, and Linda was asking for more. She watched in as Linda finished her second helping of green beans in the sauce.

Mark pulled out the cake. It was chocolate, his favorite, and offered it. Everybody wanted some. Then he pulled out some lemon sherbet and nodded to the table, everyone nodded enthusiastically, waiting for Mark's delightful desert.

When dinner was over, Lloyd and Steve went to watch TV, while Mark organized Linda and Lori, letting them help him clean up. Lois only had to load the dishwasher.

Mark then turned to the girls and said, "You've been such good helpers, let's go upstairs and I'll read you a story!"

The little girls cheered and ran up the stairs. Lois noticed that Mark was even a good "Mom", and she felt such pride for her son.

Mark read a Dr. Seuss story to the girls, asking Linda to read words that were at her level. She hadn't started school yet, but Mark had

been teaching her to sound out words, and letting her help read the stories.

After they finished that book, Mark read them the story of Beauty and the Beast, and the girls listened intently as he read different voices for each of the characters. When Belle kissed the beast and turned him back into a handsome prince, Mark accidentally said "Princess." The girls giggled and said, "Prince, a handsome prince". He smiled and tucked them in. He loved his little sisters. There were times when they could be brats, but mostly they were pretty wonderful little girls.

Lois had been listening out the door, tears of pride and joy at this delightful son who was such a wonderful mommy. Mark tucked them in, then Lois came in and gave them a good-night kiss.

The rest of the week, Mark went to Lily's during the day and played with his four friends. Each day he would dress like the other girls, picking something from Lily's wonderful wardrobe. The girls played music, danced, sang, told stories, colored, and just had a great time together. The girls all called him Marcia, and he never corrected them.

On Saturday, Lloyd insisted that Mark go with him to watch Steve's soccer match. He was hoping that Mark might get inspired by his brother, but all Mark could think of was how many times, "he" had been the ball.

The coach of the juniors' league came over to Lloyd. "Hey Woody, how's your boy doing? It's been a few years since he played on my team. Is this his little brother?"

Mark tried to be polite. "Yes sir, Steven is my older brother."

Lloyd smiled, "Hey Roy, could you give Mark a chance to try playing on your team? See how he does?"

Conversion

Marks eyes went wide with terror. "That's OK Dad, Soccer is Steve's game." Everything was Steve's game.

Coach Roy wasn't dissuaded. "Nonsense, after what Steve did, I would be a fool not to see what you can do. Come on over with me, show me what you got.

Lloyd stayed to watch Steve's game. Steve kicked a goal, putting his team ahead.

Lloyd walked over to the Juniors field and the coach told Mark to take the field.

As Mark walked out to the field, his terror multiplied. Many of these boys were the same ones that bullied him in school. He so wanted to get out of this, to just run to the sidelines and go home.

Mark went to the team he had been assigned, and immediately the taunts came, from both teams.

"Marcia wants to play with the boys. This should be fun!"

The whistle blew and the play began. The new team hadn't started learning zones yet, so very quickly there were a half-dozen boys around the ball. Then someone tripped Mark. Another boy kicked the ball into Mark's face. Boys on both teams started Mark within seconds. He couldn't curl up, but he covered his face with his hands. A kick to the gut curled him up. The boys continued to kick him for a few minutes.

The coach had been distracted talking to Lloyd then saw the cluster, "Yeah Woody, I'll need to train them to play in their zones. Right now, everybody is just trying to be as close to the ball as possible. Once we see who has what strengths, we'll teach them to play in zones, and rotate them through different zones."

Just then, the ball popped loose, rolling away from the little cluster of boys, but none of the boys seemed to have noticed. Suddenly the coach was alarmed. "Something's wrong!"

Coach Roy ran out on the field blowing his whistle. Lloyd followed. He looked for Mark in the cluster but didn't see him. As the boys broke up in response to the whistle, Lloyd looked in horror to see his son curled up on the ground, hands still covering his face. His body was curled up, and he was crying. Lloyd picked up his son and carried him off the field.

Mark cried in his father's arms. "I tried daddy, I really did, but then I fell, and they started kicking me and I couldn't move and I'm so sorry. I really tried." The crying became a wail.

When they got to the sidelines, Steve said, "I told you he was just a little sissy".

"Shut up, Steve!" The glare in Lloyd's eyes stop Steve's laughter abruptly.

By the time they got Mark home, the bruises were already beginning to show. His belly, back, thighs, arms and calves were covered with contusions. They were even on his chest.

Lois washed him off, but Mark was sleepy and couldn't stay awake. "Lloyd, you need to take him to the emergency room. Now."

Lloyd carried Mark out to the station wagon and laid him in the back with a pillow.

At the hospital, the doctor did a preliminary examination. Then he ordered x-rays. Mark was awake. The doctor talked to Mark, "You must tell the truth, did you parents do this to you?"

Conversion

Mark shook his head. "No, it was the boys on the soccer teams. Both teams started kicking me and I couldn't get up."

The doctor was doubtful. "Can you tell me the names of the boys who kicked you?"

"It's like a horror movie in my head!" Mark rattled off the first and last names of over a dozen boys. He even remembered where a few of them had kicked him.

Finally, he came out to speak with Lloyd. "He's had serious bruising to his abdomen, back, thighs, and most of his back. He may have a concussion, and he may have damage to the liver, spleen, and kidneys. Fortunately, there are no broken ribs, this time, but it appears that there was a break earlier that healed, but it did not heal well."

An hour later, Mark was in the hospital room, sedated, on monitors, with a tube in his arm.

Meanwhile, Lois had been doing laundry, and was putting Mark's clothes away. When she went to put away his underwear, she noticed something unusual in the back of the drawer. She pulled it out and realized it was a pair of girl's panties. How did Mark get them? Did he steal them from a girl? Did he make her take them off and give them to him? Was he wearing them? For now, she needed to just leave them there and see what was going on when Mark came home.

Mark was out for 3 weeks, but they kept waking him up to take his temperature, check his vitals, and give him sponge-baths. He had a catheter, so he didn't go to the bathroom, but each time they checked him, he'd wake up a few minutes, then go right back to sleep. His pulse was slow and so was his blood-pressure, but nothing critical. Gradually, the pain had eased, and he was free of

pain-killers. Finally, they decided that what damage there was had healed. Most of the bruises were gone as well.

When he got home, he had to spend another week in bed. Most of the time he just read his books. He was tired, he was still hurting. He wanted to see Lily, his best friend.

He knocked on Lily's door and Lily opened it. "Marcia, so good to see you! You were gone for weeks! Did you want to tell me about it?"

Mark smiled. "Dad tried to make me play soccer, and the coach didn't realize I was being stomped. I ended up in the hospital for 3 weeks, and then I had to stay in bed for a week. I still have some bruises." He pointed to his ribs and his belly.

Lily lifted his shirt. "Ouch, that must have really been bad if it's that bad now. It might go away in a week or two. Do you want to play?"

Mark nodded. "Yes, I miss being Marcia, but I'm hurting too much to dance. We can sing."

The two went up to Lily's room, and they sang along with the radio. There was even a new song, which Lily taught him by over-pronouncing the words. They had fun for about two hours, but Mark was wearing down quickly.

"Lily, I'm tired, I think I need to go home and rest. I'm starting to hurt, and I don't want to go back to the hospital. That's a terrible place."

Lily gave him a record. "Listen to this and learn the words, we can do the song together for Helen, Sarah, and Judy tomorrow. Wear your panties and you can be Marcia again.

Conversion

Mark smiled at that. "That would be so fun. I miss not being Marcia. It's so hard to be Mark." There was such sadness in his eyes as he shuffled home.

The next day, Mark wore the panties, and went downstairs. "Mom, I'm going over to Lily's to play. I'll be home to make dinner, just ring the bell."

Lois smiled. "OK Mark, we are having chicken tonight. Any ideas?"

Mark smiled. "Let's do chicken with spaghetti sauce! I'll jazz it up a bit. I can do fettuccine Alfredo to go with it. For a vegetable, we could do fried peppers."

Lois got a kick out of it. As Mark walked to Lily's house, Lois held the door open. She was alarmed when Lily squealed with delight and called him Marcia. Lois wondered if Lily had anything to do with those panties. She went up to Mark's room and discovered that the panties were gone. What ELSE were Mark and Lily doing together?

Lois went back to her housework. She was sewing a dress for Linda. When she finished, she decided that she really needed to check out what was going on. She went over to Lily's house. There was no car in the driveway. Was Lily at home alone with Mark? Why was she calling him Marcia? She tried the door, it was unlocked. Perhaps the best way to learn what was going on was to enter unannounced.

She heard the voices of four girls singing loudly. She followed the sound up the stairs, guessing that this would be Lily's room. She peeked through the doorway and saw 4 little girls singing like they were rock stars to a record. They were actually pretty good, but she didn't see Mark anywhere. She listened to the music until the girls finished the song. Then Lily said to the taller one, "Wow

Conversion

Marcia, you really did a great job with that one. You should sing lead on the next one."

Lois looked closer, everything about this girl was girl. She was singing with the three other girls, singing the lead vocal, and doing a great job. She was on pitch and sang into a shoe like it was a microphone. There was no bashfulness. She was confident, smiling, and performing for another girl who was sitting and listening.

She leaned forward to get a better look, and suddenly the tall girl froze, her face went blank. The other girls looked and stopped singing too. The record was playing in the background, and the girl sitting and listening turned off the volume.

Lily couldn't contain herself. "Mrs. Woodward, Marcia is an amazing singer; she is so much fun, and so pretty. We all love her, she's my bestest friend."

To her horror, Liz realized that "Marcia" was actually Mark, her son.

Lois just froze. The girl she saw in front of her was a girl in every way, cute, pretty, silly, and indistinguishable from any other of the girls in the room. She didn't know what to do. She was calm. "Mark, change your clothes, it's time to go home."

She watched all of the life, the joy, the happiness, drain from his face. His shoulders slumped, his walk went from a cheerful dance to a shuffle. Mark went into the bathroom with his clothes. When he came out, he was dressed in blue jeans, a baggy T-shirt, and his sneakers were untied. He looked so sad, so helpless, so hopeless.

As he got ready to leave, Lois watched all the girls come up and hug him, they were so nice to him, and all of them called him Marcia. They couldn't wait to sing with him again. For a moment, there was a spark of life, then it drained out.

Lois had to investigate. "Mark, wait for me downstairs, I need to talk to the girls for a minute."

As Mark trudged downstairs to the door, Lois turned to the girls. "Girls, I have to know, did Mark make you dress him up? Has he tried to kiss you or touch your privates?"

All four of the girls shook their heads. Sarah spoke, "Why would she do that, she's just one of us girls. She's really nice and fun to be with. She didn't want to wear the dress at first, but when we promised not to tell her brother, she finally tried it on. She was scared at first, but once she got the wig on, she was so happy, she was having so much fun. She's been Marcia ever since."

Lois snapped, "Mark is a boy! He has a penis! He's not a girl!"

Sarah didn't back down. "Ma'am, I don't know if she has a penis or not, I've never seen it, but she doesn't act anything like any stupid boy I know. She acts like a girl. She's not even a tomboy like Melanie."

Lily was more contrite. "I'm sorry Mrs. Woodward; it was my idea to let him wear a dress if he wanted to. He is such a girl in so many other ways. All the boys at school hate him, but most of the girls like him. He's just really nice, polite, and sweet. And he's so pretty too."

Lois held her hand up. "No more dressing him up as a girl. He's not a Barbie doll, he's a boy, and he shouldn't be wearing girls' clothes. If you don't stop, he can't play with you anymore. Do you understand?"

Lily nodded reluctantly. "Yes Mrs. Woodward, I understand. No more dressing him up. But he can still play with us?"

Conversion

Lois nodded slowly. She had just gotten her son home from the hospital, the result of the last time he played with a bunch of boys. "I guess so, but no more dressing him as a girl, OK?"

As Lois arrived at the bottom of the stairs where Mark was waiting, his expression clearing conveyed his fears. He didn't want his father to find out. He knew his dad would belt him.

When they got back to the house, Lois shut the door. "OK MARCIA!", contempt dripping in the name,, "If you want to be a girl, you can do all the housework like a girl! That means cooking, cleaning, laundry, cleaning the bathrooms, and even helping to watch Linda. You'll find out that being a girl isn't so much fun after all!"

To her astonishment, Mark smiled, he suddenly looked happy. "Thank you, mom! I'll be a really good housewife, I can help you with everything."

Lois wanted to kill that enthusiasm. "But no more dressing as a girl, understand?"

Mark looked sad for a minute, then said, "OK, but can I still help you with the housework? Can you also teach me how to sew?"

Lois's jaw just dropped. She was going to have to load him up with so much work that he hated it, then he would never want to be a girl again.

"Fine, you can start with the laundry. Pick up all the dirty clothes in each of the rooms, put them in the hamper, and bring it downstairs."

About 15 minutes later, Mark was dragging down the huge hamper full of clothes, lifting it and lowering it a couple steps at a time. Then he took it into the laundry room. He started sorting the

laundry into whites, brights, colors and darks, and delicates. Lois watched as he figured out each item, going through the whole hamper in about 10 minutes. "Mom, I should do whites first, but I need some bleach, Stevie and Daddy have skid marks and I need to scrub them out. Then I'll put the detergent on the hard spots."

Lois was astonished, "You know how to do laundry?"

Mark smiled, "I've been watching you do it for years. I was afraid if I asked to help, you would think I was a sissy and wouldn't let me. I guess you know by now, I'm not at all like Steve."

Lois gave him some bleach and watched as he put some in a cup and dipped the skid marks into the bleach. Then he used some liquid detergent to presoak these trouble spots. He reached up and set the washer on hot, then put all the whites into the wash, added the correct amount of detergent, and he started the washer.

Lois handed him a sponge and a can of cleanser. "While that's running, you can clean the upstairs bathroom.", that was her least favorite chore. Mark smiled, grabbed the can and the sponge, and ran up the stairs.

He was done before the laundry was. "Mom, would you take a look, I want to make sure I didn't miss anything!"

Lois came up to inspect. He had washed the sinks, the faucets were shining, the shower tiles had been scrubbed down, and the ring in the tub was gone. She lifted the lid and was surprised to see that the entire bowl was clean, including the outside of the rim. She noticed that even the floor had been scrubbed clean of the yellow stains where the boys had missed. "You cleaned the floor here too?"

Mark nodded, "Steve's a real pig, he can't aim worth beans. I don't know why he doesn't just sit, like I do."

Lois smiled, "You did a great job Mark, it looks great. Now you need to get back to the laundry."

Mark went downstairs and shifted the laundry. He moved the whites from the washer to the dryer and loaded the colors into the washer. He added a cup of liquid detergent, shut the lid, set the temperature to warm wash, cool rinse, and started it. "Did you want me to do the downstairs bathroom now?"

Lois nodded. "Yes, this is a good time to do it, you have about 40 minutes before the dryer is done and you need to start folding."

Mark smiled. "Good, I can even get started on dinner."

Over the next week, Mark quickly learned to do all of the domestic chores. He even learned to iron his father's shirts, using lots of starch, and even ironed his mom's pleated skirt. Mark was picking up all of the housework. Lois was down to just inspecting the finished work. Mark didn't complain, and even seemed enthusiastic. He seemed to enjoy being a housewife. Unfortunately, Lloyd was beginning to notice and was starting to make rude comments.

After a few more days, Lois decided Mark could handle the chores. "I'm going shopping with Linda and Lori to get some clothes. You can watch the house. Vacuum the rugs and mop the floor while I'm gone. We'll be gone about four hours. We'll be back in time for dinner.

With the house all to himself, he mopped the floors, then he went up to his room. He missed being one of the girls. All these new chores had given him less time with Lily and his other friends. The school wasn't letting him play with the girls anymore. He was beginning to feel very lonely.

Conversion

He went up to his room. He pulled out the panties he had hidden between the mattresses of his bed. Five times, Lois had thrown out his panties, and each time he rescued them from the trash. He had to get more creative about hiding his clothes.

He had finished folding the laundry and was putting it away. He went into his parent's room and put away his dad's whites and casual clothes. Then he put away his mother's lingerie, the pretty bras, her girdles, and six pairs of panties. He imagined what it might be like to wear a girdle, stockings, and a pretty Sunday Morning dress.

Mark noticed that his mom seemed to change clothes often. In the daytime, she would wear a shift, and at night, before daddy came home, she would change into something dressier.

He held up a pretty dress and looked in the mirror. He couldn't wear Lily's dresses anymore, and it made him very sad. He began to wonder what the pretty dress would look like. He was quite surprised to find, when he tried it on, that it almost fit. It was still a bit large for him around the waist, but it came to about 2 inches above the knee. He twirled as he looked in the full-length mirror. He looked pretty, but older. He took off the dress, put his own clothes back on.

Soon, each time Lois left the house with the girls, he would try on one of the dresses from the dirty clothes. They smelled like her perfume. Then he started wearing the shifts while he was cleaning. He would listen for the sound of the car door, and run upstairs and shed the sheath, and drop it in the hamper while Lois wrestled with his sisters.

One day, Lois took the girls shopping. She had gotten to the mall, when she realized that she had left her wallet on the dresser. She went back to get it, leaving the girls in the car, since she was going

right back. Mark had changed into his shift, and was vacuuming the rug, so he didn't hear Lois come in.

Lois just stared as she watched the slender young girl, vacuuming the rug, wearing her sheath dress and a pair of 2-inch pumps. She was graceful, pretty, and then she realized it was Mark. Lois also had a wig, nearly black hair, but Mark had found it and was wearing it. If Lois didn't know that was Mark, she would never have seen anything other than a pretty girl. Lois went upstairs to get her wallet.

Mark shut off the vacuum and heard his mother up in her room. He flew up the stairs and shut the door to his room. He had locked the door and was out of the dress and heels in a matter of seconds. It took a few minutes to get dressed. When he came out the door, Lois was waiting for him.

"Mark, you have to stop stealing my clothes. It's bad enough that you wear them, but I don't want you STEALING!"

Mark was stunned, "Then where will I get pretty clothes?" He covered his mouth, not believing he had just said that.

Lois realized that this was a dilemma. "You shouldn't be wearing my clothes at all. I was going to give that one to good-will anyway, so I guess you can wear it, but you have to wash it. Don't let your father find it or you'll get the belt for sure."

Shopping

Lois had been thinking about getting a job. Lloyd was making good money, but she wanted some of her own spending money. Besides, Mark was doing all the housework, and Lois hated housework. A neighbor had agreed to take the girls three days a week if Lois would watch hers three days a week. She could at least get a part-time job.

Lois told Mark she was shopping for some work clothes. Mark smiled, "Can I come too? I've finished the housework for today, and I could help you look more modern."

Lois couldn't believe her ears, but then she remembered the times when she had come home from shopping, and the girls showed off their new clothes. Mark knew what went well together, what worked, and why. He even made a few kind remarks about her own choices.

The two went to the store together. Lois was looking at house-dresses, when Mark pulled a short black skirt, rust colored satin blouse, and a maroon blazer from various racks. "Try these Mom".

Lois was a bit stunned to realize that Mark had not only picked out a very refined look, but everything was in her correct sizes. "OK Mark, I'll try it on, since you were nice enough to pick it out."

Lois went to the dressing room and put on the new outfit. It wasn't what she would have chosen. The skirt seemed a bit short, about 3 inches above her knees, and the satin blouse seemed over the top, and the cropped jacket just seemed like overkill, yet when she had everything on, she turned and looked into the mirror and was stunned. It was a perfect look for the office. She came out to show it to Mark.

"Oh mom, that is so perfect for the office, you really need to get it. The rust and maroon make your hair glow, and the darker colors go

with your autumn complexion. Did you want to try something else?"

Lois was dumbfounded, "Yes, can you pick out two more skirts and two more blouses, and maybe another jacket?"

Mark was delighted. Within minutes he had selected another combination, "Try these. You should be able to mix and match and get some great combinations. While you're trying that one, I'll get you another one."

Lois tried on the second ensemble, this was a mauve blouse, dark brown skirt, and a black jacket. Lois could easily see herself working in an office in these clothes. When she came out to model them, Mark had a third combination ready to go.

Mark was delighted. "Mom, that looks so lovely on you, sophisticated and classy, but not old fashioned. But we should look some more and that way you can pick what you like best."

For the next two hours, they shopped, Mark picking out wonderful outfits for office, and Lois trying on each and being overwhelmed by how great everything looked. Her son actually said "lovely"?!?

The hardest thing for Lois was narrowing down the choices, yet Mark helped there too. Eventually he picked out three outfits that could be combined in different ways to give two dozen different wonderful looks. Lois and Mark agreed they wouldn't tell anyone that Mark had picked out her wardrobe.

That night, Lois modeled the outfits for Lloyd, who was totally impressed with all of the looks. "You could easily work in my company's offices. Heck you could be a model in my store! You look totally professional, and young and beautiful.

Lois applied for a few jobs in the area and landed a job on her third interview. She would be helping a doctor's office collect from insurance companies. Since many of these companies had local offices, she might have to go into the field. She made such a good impression, that they were ready to start her that day.

Lois put a few of her older dresses in the donation bag. She would take them to the charity in a few days. Then she noticed that a few items were missing. She found one of the dresses in the back of Mark's closet, under a pile of dirty clothes. She decided not to make a big deal about it.

Mark was doing all the housework and was only getting a meager allowance. She couldn't really call it stealing if he was providing such wonderful service, and his meals were so much cheaper than eating at a restaurant. Mark seemed to be able to create well-balanced meals that were delicious for less than two dollars a day. Even taking the family to McDonalds would cost more than 12 dollars for the six of them.

As a test, she put a pair of low heels into the donation bag. Sure enough, three days later, they were gone. There was no question, Marcia was helping herself to the donation bag. She did notice that a pair of panties were missing? Marcia again?

Over the next year, Lois would notice things disappearing from the bag. She even put a new pair of panties into the bag, and a pair of pantyhose without runs. They were gone in a day or so. She decided to keep it their little secret.

Exposed!

Lois had gone to work, the kids were out, and Steve had gone to the field to practice. Marcia was happily doing the housework, in her shift and heels. She had shortened the skirt of the dress so that it looked better. She looked really cute. She was also wearing

Conversion

mom's wig. She was vacuuming when Steve walked through the door.

Steve looked for Mark. Mark was supposed doing a bunch of housework, but he seemed to have disappeared. So, who was this cute girl who was vacuuming the rugs? He started to move forward to check her out, maybe see if he could get a date, then he realized that it was Mark. He ran out of the house before Mark could even react.

As Mark finished the housework, he decided that he needed to wait until AFTER he was done vacuuming before dressing up as Marcia. This was twice he had been caught in the act, and Steve was not going to let it drop.

That night, at the dinner table, Steve couldn't wait to reveal his discovery. Mark had made a pot roast, potatoes, French cut green beans in tomato sauce, and some candied carrots. Even Linda and Lori ate their vegetables without hesitation.

Lloyd was delighted with the meal, "That was wonderful Mark. Those green beans are like your grandma makes."

Mark smiled. "Yes, I remembered them from Thanksgiving last year. I didn't have the recipe, but I guess this is a close approximation. Onions, bacon, green beans and tomato paste.

Steve gloated. "Oh yes, Mark is quite the Suzy homemaker. Isn't she, MARCIA?"

Lois was stunned. "What do YOU know about Marcia?" She wished she hadn't spoken.

Steve smiled big. "I know, I came home from practice all hot and sweaty. There was this really cute girl vacuuming the floor. She was cute, so I decided to check her out. But when she turned, I

Page 38

realized it was MARCIA! Oh dad, you should have seen it, she was so cute in her short little mini-dress, heels, and long flowing wig. I almost grabbed her ass, before I realized it was Mark! Or is that MARCIA?"

Mark couldn't help himself, he smiled each time Steve called him Marcia. If Steve was going to blab, maybe it was better to have it out in the open!

Lloyd was stone-faced. "Mark, is this true? Were you dressed up as a girl?"

Suddenly Mark was terrified. "Yes sir."

Lloyd grabbed Mark by the arm, "Upstairs, now. It's time for a bible lesson."

Mark began to sob. Everyone at the table knew that a "Bible Lesson" from Lloyd usually ended with the belt. Lloyd was a Christian Conservative and loved to use the Bible to explain the sin being committed, and the punishment being dished out. Many of these "sins" were verses taken out of context and were bad translations. Mark knew this but knew better than to argue with his father when he was getting a "Bible Lesson".

Lloyd opened his King James Bible to Deuteronomy. "Read Chapter 22, verse 5 please."

Mark read, terrified. "The woman shall not wear that which pertaineth unto a man, neither shall a man put on a woman's garment: for all that do so are abomination unto the Lord."

Lloyd growled. "Do you know what an abomination is, Mark?"

Mark cowered. "No sir."

Conversion

Lloyd's voice was calm, "An abomination is something so terrible, God hates it so much, that he will kill them for being an abomination. I love you Mark, and I don't want you to be an abomination. I don't want God to Destroy you. I have to make sure you never do it again."

He pulled off his necktie and bound Mark's hands then pushed him over the foot of the bed. The high wooden slat cut into his stomach. He pulled down Mark's pants all the way to his ankles.

Lloyd unbuckled his belt. "I'm going to be merciful. I should give you thirty-nine lashes, like our Lord received. If you promise you'll never do it again, I'll only do 20, but you have to be still and take your punishment. Do you promise?"

Mark was terrified, so he nodded his head. He'd never had more than 5, and they were so painful he couldn't sit for a week. 20 lashes were going to hurt that much worse.

Lloyd stood back, measuring the length of the lash, so it would just wrap around the area being hit. The belt was smooth, and the leather was firm, but there were no metal parts to cut or nick. "Son, this hurts me more than it hurts you, but it has to be done."

The first lash whipped across the flesh of his butt. Mark screamed out in pain, crying, but he held his hands down, folded in front of him, praying aloud, "Lord forgive me, I am an evil sinner and I repent my sins".

The second lash came down on his thighs, leaving a 1-inch wide red welt, but no bleeding.

Mark screamed again, "Lord forgive me, I am an evil sinner and I repent my sins."

Conversion

This was repeated for 5 more strokes, each more intense, over his back, buttocks, thighs and knees. Finally, Mark was just crying incoherently.

Lloyd shouted, "Enough! Be silent! I don't want to listen to your whimpering prayers, say it silently to yourself instead."

Lloyd swung again, Mark bit his lip so hard he was bleeding, but he said nothing. It hurt so bad.

Somewhere around the 8th or 9th stroke, something strange happened. It was as if Mark was no longer in his body. He stopped struggling, his muscles relaxed, and he didn't even react as the belt came down, searing his flesh with what should have been incredible pain. Instead, there was a calm, a surrender. Mark gave himself up to the pain and stopped screaming. It was as if his mind had left his body, he was watching himself be whipped, he could see the welts, but he felt only a calm relaxed serenity.

Suddenly, it was over. Lloyd nodded. "I'm proud of you son, you took your punishment like a man. Now don't ever let me catch you in a dress again, or I swear I'll do the whole 39 lashes." Lloyd stood up and walked out of the room, going down the stairs.

Mark straightened up, untied his hands with his teeth, and pulled his pants up. It hurt so bad. He just went into his room, took off his clothes, and laid on his stomach.

An hour later, his mother came up. She was horrified to see the bruises on his back, butt, and thighs. Mark just laid there, still. Lois started to put some soothing lotion on his welts.

Mark cried, "Daddy wants me to stop being Marcia. I can't. I wish I was dead".

Conversion

Lois began to realize how real Marcia was for her son. Even with the threat of another beating, Mark still wanted to be Marcia.

The next day, Lois took Mark to church with her, while the rest of the family went with Lloyd. Lois wanted to see if the pastor could talk some sense into Mark. Even early in the morning, the hot July sun burned down on the car. Mark remembered his grandfather's car. It had air conditioning. This car was just hot.

Lois went into Pastor Jim's office with Mark. "Pastor Jim, Mark has been acting strangely and I think he might need some counseling. Could you talk to him, and maybe make a recommendation to me about what to do?"

Pastor Jim smiled. "Of course, what seems to be the problem?" Lois was uncertain. Could she be making matters worse? "He's been acting like a girl all summer, even dressing up in girls' clothes."

The pastor smiled. "Lois, could you give me a few minutes alone with him?"

Lois reluctantly left the room.

The second the door was shut; the Pastor Jim's kind smile was gone. "Mark, do you really think you are a girl?"

Mark nodded. "I'm not at all good at being a boy, but I like playing with my friends, who are all girls, and I like doing housework, and I like being pretty."

The pastor growled, "But you're NOT a girl, are you? You have a penis. That makes you a boy."

Conversion

Mark nodded. "It's not much of a penis, but I have one. The boys make fun of me because it's so tiny. I'm much smaller than Steve, he's about four times bigger."

Pastor Jim sat at his desk. "Come here, Mark. You're lying, show it to me," he growled.

Mark just cowered.

Pastor Jim leered, breathing heavily as he pulled down Mark's pants and underwear in one quick pull. He was shocked. There between his legs was the smallest penis he had ever seen. It was only a half-inch long. He grabbed the boy's crotch. There were no testicles. He stroked the penis, and it grew to about an inch. The boy was terrified.

Pastor Jim sneered angrily. "Pull up your pants boy. What are you doing exposing yourself to other boys in the first place?"

Mark was about to cry. "When I go to the bathroom, I sit to pee. They've taken the doors off the boys' stalls, and the boys pull me off the toilet to make fun of my tiny thingy. Then they show me what they have, bigger with a pouch underneath. I'm some sort of a freak."

Pastor Jim almost felt sorry for the boy. Maybe he would be better off as a girl. Then he hardened. "Nonetheless, you have a penis, therefore you are a boy. Have you read Deuteronomy 22, verse 5?"

Mark's eyes widened in terror "Yes, my father made me read it last night. He said I was an abomination, and he whipped me 20 times with his belt."

"He did, did he? Let me see your back-side." For the second time, Pastor Jim tugged down the pants. The welts and bruises were

obvious. Clearly the boy had been whipped, hard and many times. He leered, admiring the welts. "Spare the rod, spoil the child, I say. Good for your father. You're not going to wear dresses anymore are you? Pull your pants up boy, you look disgusting!"

Mark pulled up his pants a second time and tucked in his shirt. He shook his head, "But I can't be a boy either!"

Pastor Jim was fed up. "You don't want to go to HELL, do you? Do you know what hell is like?"

Marks eyes widened again "Yes, fire and brimstone, horrible smells, everybody burning and screaming for all of eternity." Little did Mark know he was quoting Dante's Inferno, not the Bible.

The pastor smiled. "You've listened well, there may be hope for you yet! Why don't you go to Sunday School while I talk to your mother?"

Mark left the office and told Lois that the pastor wanted to talk to her alone. Lois entered the room and sat across from the pastor. "Pastor, as you can see, he's very confused and troubled. I was wondering if you could recommend someone who could help him?"

Pastor Jim opened his desk drawer and pulled out a card. "This man has had some luck with faggots and sissies, but I'll tell you now, it doesn't look good. May I ask one question? Was there anything unusual about the pregnancies?"

Lois looked down, then looked the pastor in the eye. "Pastor, I've lost 3 babies who were still-born prematurely. My mother had lost 2, and Lloyd's mother had lost two. When I was pregnant with Mark, the doctor recommended a medication to prevent me from losing the baby, it was called DES. It had a lot of estrogen in it. Do you think that's why he's so feminine?"

Conversion

Pastor Jim was curious, but he had a sermon to preach and didn't want to encourage Mark. "I'm sorry Mrs. Woodward, I need to prepare for the service now, if you will excuse me."

Mark didn't go to Sunday School, he went to his father's car, and locked himself in. "If hell is terrible, then maybe this hot car will help me feel what it's like and make me want to stop being a girl."

Mark sat in the car, reading his bible. He read the whole book of Deuteronomy from his King James Bible. There were so many rules, so many laws, so many abominations, so many things that were unclean. How could anybody not end up in hell? Soon, the heat of the hot July sun beating down on the black car, with the black upholstery was too much. He took his jacket off and fell asleep.

Mark had been asleep in the car for almost forty minutes, when the security guard walking the parking lot and directing traffic spotted Mark's white shirt in the back seat. The car was locked, and he couldn't get it open. He called for the police on his radio. Within ten minutes, the police car pulled up next to the officer. The police officer used a thin strip of metal to open the car door. Mark was still alive, but he was not waking up.

The officer said, "I'll take him to the hospital now, you tell his parents where he is."

It took 10 minutes to get to the nearest hospital. The officer carried the unconscious boy into the emergency room. "We found him in a hot car, we got him out, but I don't know how long he's been there. He's not waking up."

The doctor started the examination immediately. "Pupils fixed and dilated, unresponsive, heart rate is 104, BP is 90/60. Appears to be heat stroke. We need to cool him off.". The nurse took off the

Page 45

shirt and gasped. The bruises from the whipping were fully visible. She took off his pants and saw that the welts went from his neck to his calves.

The doctor hesitated. "We can't deal with that now, we have to get his temperature down. His temperature is 106, if it goes up another degree, we'll lose him. Get me some blankets, and a bowl of ice cubes in water. We have to get him cool as quickly as possible."

Within 2 minutes, they had ice in a small bowl. They added water, and the doctor immersed the towel. "Let's hope this doesn't shock him too badly."

The doctor then spread the cold blanket across Mark's chest, and another across his legs. Then he slowly poured some additional icy water over the blankets. He watched for a reaction, but Mark wasn't moving. The nurse said a silent prayer for God to help this little boy. She knew that he could either die or come back quite suddenly.

After 15 minutes, they put him on his stomach, covered his backside with the cold towels, and the nurse took his temperature rectally. Nobody wanted to risk that he would come to suddenly and bite into the thermometer. The mercury and glass were far too dangerous. His temperature was down to 102, his heart rate was up to 60, and his blood pressure was 110/60. Mark was coming back, but what was coming back? Would there be anything left of his brain after being so overheated for so long.

Suddenly, Mark's arms started flailing, he pulled the icy blanket off himself. They rolled him back onto his back. His eyes were still closed, but he was fighting the blankets the doctor was trying to add. Suddenly Mark's eyes popped open.

"I'm so cold, shivering!" He pushed the cold blankets off of himself.

Conversion

Finally, the doctor put a dry blanket over Mark. "Looks like you're back. We thought we'd lost you for a few minutes. I need to ask you a few questions."

Mark smiled and nodded, "OK Doctor, I'll answer as well as I can."

The doctor asked, "What's your name?"

Mark smiled, "Marcia … I mean Mark". His eyes widened with fear. He had just told this stranger about Marcia.

The doctor was more interested in Mark's cognitive functions. "Do you know what day it is?"

Mark smiled. "Sunday. Oh no, I need to get back to church, my mom will be worried!"

The doctor asked where he lived, and Mark gave his address, and named the town as Lincoln, Nebraska.

The doctor could now ask some other questions. "How did you get those bruises on your back?"

Mark was so ashamed. "My dad took a belt to me. He didn't like that I looked like a girl."

The doctor nodded, "Oh, that makes sense. But you're not a girl, are you?"

Mark hesitated, refusing to answer.

The doctor looked him in the eye, he could see the fear. "You have a penis. It's small, but it's there. So, you're a boy, right?"

Mark looked so sad. "I guess so. I'm really bad at being a boy."

Conversion

The doctor smiled "Some boys don't get bigger until they are older. Then puberty comes and they get bigger, they get their testes, and they get their man voices. They get taller and stronger, like your father."

Mark almost cried, "No!"

The doctor smiled. "Didn't your father explain all this? How old are you?"

Mark looked so sad. "I'm 11, sir."

The doctor sat across from Mark. "You're at that age when you will soon be going through puberty. Your voice will get deeper, you'll grow a beard and start shaving, you'll grow hair on your arms and legs, and you'll start to like girls."

Mark giggled. "I already like girls! My best friends are Lily, Sarah, Helen, and Judy. We're best buddies."

The doctor was thoughtful. "Your friends will be changing too, they will be growing breasts, and curves, and you will want to kiss them."

Mark looked worried "You mean like I want to kiss Davey Jones of the Monkees?"

The doctor stopped smiling. "Are you saying you're attracted to boys?"

Mark nodded. "I don't know why. The boys in my school are so mean to me, calling me sissy and fairy, but some of the boys are really cute. I just wish they weren't so mean."

"And your father whipped you with a belt for liking boys?"

Mark shook his head. "Oh no, sir! He whipped me because my brother caught me dressing like a girl."

The doctor stopped short. "Do you want to be a girl?"

Mark smiled. "Yes, I want to be like my other friends, grow my hair long, wear pretty clothes, and not have to play sports with the boys. They always beat me up."

The doctor looked at the file. "That's right, you were in here before. The boys had kicked you on the soccer field?"

Mark nodded. "I had to stay in the hospital for three weeks and stay in bed for another week. It was a while ago."

The doctor was concerned, but didn't want to alarm the boy. "I can see why you don't want to play with boys. Does your mother beat you?"

Mark shook his head. "No, she's really nice. She knew about Marcia first, but she didn't tell my daddy, because she knew he would be mad."

The doctor was curious. "Marcia, you used that name when you first came to. That's the name you use when you are pretending to be a girl?"

Mark giggled. "No, Mark is the name I use when I'm pretending to be a boy."

The doctor, laughed for a second, marked on his chart. GID for "Gender Identity Disorder". It was at the end of the last line. He didn't know what to do about it, because telling the father could mean another beating.

Conversion

Lois was crying. "Oh, Mark, I was so worried about you. Why did you do that?"

Mark cried too. "I'm sorry momma, the Minister told me I was going to hell, and I figured if I sat in the hot car for a while, I might be scared enough to stop being Marcia."

Lloyd went cold. "Did it work?"

Mark nodded. "The funny thing is that when I fell asleep, I dreamed I went to heaven and talked to Jesus. He was so nice. He told me I had to come back because I needed to do something. It was so bright and so pretty. I even saw Uncle Alec and Uncle Corney."

Lloyd was distant. "Well, I hope that made you want to go to heaven instead of hell!"

Mark was contrite. "Yes daddy, I want to go to heaven."

Lois tried to be loving. "Why don't we go home, and you can make some French toast, bacon, and eggs for the whole family."

Mark smiled. "Scrambled eggs with cheese!"

The doctor stopped. "I need to talk to your mother for a few minutes. Why don't you wait in the lobby with your father?"

After the family left, the Lois was worried. "What's wrong doctor? Why didn't you want my husband here?"

The doctor was upset. "Your husband whipped your son with a belt! There were bruises all over his backside from his neck to his ankles. If it happens again, I will have to report him to child services. Your son is very confused. He thinks he is a girl, and he might be homosexual. You should get him treatment right away. I

was afraid that if I told you this in front of your husband, he might beat the boy again."

Lois nodded "I caught him dressed as a girl with his friends a while ago. I tried to punish him by making him do all the housework, but he seems to really enjoy it. He does a better job than I do, and he even takes care of his baby sister. He acts like a girl."

The doctor shook his head "Mrs. Woodward, your son is suffering from Gender Identity Disorder. It's like a psychosis. Even though he knows he has a penis, he thinks he's a girl."

Lois smiled. "Have you seen his penis? It's tiny, barely there. He doesn't have the other boy parts like his brother did. It's almost as if his penis was an accident. He's never acted like a boy. He doesn't fight, he doesn't play sports, he doesn't even jostle with his brother. When he was a toddler, the other boys would take his toys and he didn't even fight to get them back. He was more like my daughters than my oldest son."

The doctor crossed his arms. "Nevertheless Mrs. Woodward, this is potentially a very dangerous condition. Many boys with GID try to commit suicide. He needs a good therapist who will make him see reality."

Lois nodded. "I talked to my minister, he gave me the name of a therapist." She showed him the card.

The doctor nodded. "Yes, I know of him. He's a good choice. He should be able to help your son"

Lois held out a hand. "Thank you doctor and thank you for not telling my husband."

Conversion

Mark had to stay in the hospital for a few more days to make sure there was no brain damage, and then he was finally allowed to go home.

IdRaHaJe

When they got home, Lois pulled Lloyd into the bedroom while Mark made the brunch.

She shut the door behind them. "Lloyd, we need to talk. The doctor saw all those bruises from the whipping you gave Mark. He told me that if you did it again, he would have to report you! You have to promise me that you won't whip him again!"

Lloyd was defensive. "I used a belt and I only gave him 20 lashes. Pop used a razor strap and I often got 30 lashes or more. It hurt like hell, but I learned my lessons."

Lois shook her head. "That might have been OK 30 years ago, but it's not OK anymore. I saw those bruises. Mark looked terrible. It hurt so much to see him hurting so badly, to see all those welts, those bruises, and that sadness."

Lloyd nodded. "What should I do. I can't let him go running around in dresses. He could be arrested, or the boys might beat him up. Remember what happened at soccer practice?"

Lois winced. "I talked to the Minister, and he gave me a card. There is a therapist who might be able to help."

Lloyd shook his head. "No shrinks. I'll call Pop and see if he has any ideas that don't involve whippings."

That afternoon, Lloyd went into his den and locked the door. He dialed the phone and flipped the egg timer.

Earnest answered the phone. "Hello?"

Lloyd yelled into the phone, "Hi Pop, it's me."

Conversion

The other voice was delighted "Buddy? Is that you? We just got back from church, did you want me to put Grandma on too?"

Lloyd's voice got softer. "Pop, Steve caught Mark wearing a dress and doing housework like a girl. I'm worried about him Pop, Mark is acting like a little sissy."

Pop's voice was quieter too "Oh, that's bad news. We need to save his soul and MAKE him repent. I think I know what to do. We can send him to a Christian Summer camp. It's called IdRaHaJe, short for I'd Rather Have Jesus. He would be with some other good Christian boys, and he would be getting some good Christian guidance. I've sent some of my other grandsons there, and it really helped them. I'll even pay the fees. I'll mail you the brochure and packing list. I'll make the call as soon as you hang up. I'm sure they will make room for the grandson of one of their key donors."

Lloyd smiled. "That would be great Pop! Send me the details. I see that our three minutes are almost up. I'll get off now, so we don't get charged for another three minutes. Bye Pop, love you!"

"Why don't you have Lois bring the kids to Colorado? We have Anne's kids for a week, and it might be more fun for all of them to have company."

Lloyd smiled "That's a great idea Pop, I'll call you with the details after I talk to Lois. Loves you!"

Pop laughed "Loves you buddy, bye" and he hung up.

Lloyd went down to the breakfast. It smelled wonderful. Maybe it was OK if Mark kept cooking and helping around the house. They have men chefs after all.

Lloyd sat at the head of the table, Lois sat at the foot, Steve sat next to Lori and Mark sat next to Linda. They said their family

Conversion

prayer. "God is great, God is good, and we thank him for our food. Amen"

After everyone had been served, Lloyd smiled. "I've got some good news. Grandpa wants to send Mark to Summer camp. It's a camp in the mountains. For two whole weeks!"

Steve whined, "How come Mark gets to go to Summer camp and I don't? He's just a silly sissy!"

Lloyd turned to his oldest son. "Steve, you have baseball practice and soccer practice, and soon you will be getting ready for football season. Mark doesn't like sports, so I thought I'd give him a chance to spend some time with some boys and girls his own age without getting hurt."

Steve giggled. "Yeah, he can sleep with the GIRLS!"

Mark smiled for a moment before he saw his father give him a threatening look. He'd just had one beating, it was too soon for another one.

Lloyd nodded. "Pop will tell me when Mark can go. Meanwhile, he invited the family to go to Colorado for a week and spend some time with Anne's kids."

Lois shook her head "Lloyd, I can't go for a week, I have my job, and Steve has all those sports you just mentioned, and your mom is too old to be watching two little girls."

Lloyd thought for a minute. "How about this? We'll drive down to Fort Collins Friday night, and drive back Sunday afternoon after church. It's only a three-hour drive, and we could have the week-end at Pops. Mark could stay the whole week with Russ and Will. Then the next week, we could drive down for the week-end and then take Mark home with us."

Lois smiled. "I do like your parents, and I really miss Anne. We can do it, but we have to leave right after church on Sunday both weekends. I don't want to miss any work and I don't want to be tired on Monday morning."

Lloyd nodded. "It's settled then, I'll call him later to tell him the good news."

After the brunch, Mark and Lois cleared the table. It seemed that Mark was still happy to do the housework, even if he couldn't be Marcia anymore. Mark felt like he was a spy. He was still doing the housework, but he had to keep it a secret that he was still Marcia. No matter what those other people said, he knew that the person he really was, his True Self, was Marcia, and that wasn't going to change.

Grandpa's place.

The following Friday, the family started the drive. They left at about 2pm, as soon as Lois got off work. They drove the whole way as fast as they could, making only two rest stops over the 7-hour drive. They made good time and were at Pops by 9pm. Grandma had a nice dinner waiting for them, meatloaf and mashed potatoes.

Everybody ate and then went to bed. Mark was bunking at Grandma's house with Will and Steve was bunking with Russ. Lori and Linda went to Unc's house with Lois and Lloyd. Anne, Lloyd's baby sister, the youngest of the 4 sisters, and her husband Tom were also at Unc's. Unc was their mother's brother, so they could step outside and smoke if they needed. Anne had been a bit rebellious in college, and rebelled against her Pop's strict rules against smoking, drinking, dancing, and playing cards. Sometimes, it seemed to Anne, that Pop had rules against anything that was fun. Even at 30, she still tried to avoid her father's judgement.

Conversion

The next morning, Russ woke up Steve, Mark and Will. "Grandpa is going to read us Bible Stories". Russ loved to listen to Grandpa read Bible stories. He loved the way Grandpa would act so astonished at what he was reading, each time he read it. Steve told Russ to go away, he didn't want to listen to Bible stories.

Mark just didn't want Grandpa judging him. Had his dad told Grandpa about Marcia?

Grandpa read the story of Shadrack, Meshack, and Abednego, in the fiery hot furnace, how the angel of the Lord protected them from any harm. Mark thought, "Maybe God sent an angel to protect me while I was in the car last Sunday?"

On Sunday, all of the families went to Grandpa's church. In Sunday School, both Mark and Russ were wearing shorts. They were so cute, and they knew all of the songs and both sang loudly, in tune, and on pitch. Later, when the teacher read the Bible story, each time she asked a question, both Mark and Russ knew the right answers and blurted them out. Steve sulked in the back of the room. Will was giggling in the back with another boy.

When the lesson was over, Mark and Russ went to play with the girls and played house with them. They were so sweet, taking care of the baby dolls, cooking, and having tea with the other girls.

When class was over, Ernest came to pick up the boys. The teacher couldn't resist the urge to tease a little. "Ernest, Stevie and Will are such typical boys, but Mark and Russ are such adorable little girls, you must be so proud!" It was only when she saw the look of terror in Mark's eyes that she realized she needed to stop immediately. "They are just so polite and well-behaved."

When they got home from church, they changed out of their dressy clothes, and both Russ and Mark asked grandma if they could help

Conversion

in the kitchen. She had them both peel potatoes. They laughed and sang together, they were having a wonderful time. Lois and Anne smiled at the two boys.

Ann smiled. "Russ is so sweet, and he has become quite the housewife. He has become a really good cook, and he does all of the housework. I love that I can go work in an office and interact with adults again. He's so sweet, he should have been born a girl."

Lois was suddenly fascinated. "Mark is like that too! I caught him at the neighbor's house wearing a dress, so I made him start doing housework. I thought he would hate it, but he seems to enjoy it, and he is very good at it."

Ann nodded. "Russ was wearing my clothes. I found a stash of clothes in his closet, so I made him do housework. He's really good at it, and I get to work. A few times, I gave come home early while he was vacuuming, and he was wearing my dress, wig, and boots. I can't wear heels, or I bet he'd be wearing those too. He actually makes a very pretty girl!"

Lois paused. "Does your husband know?"

Ann laughed, "Oh yes, he knows. He doesn't like it, but he knows. Of course, Tom isn't exactly Mr. Macho either. He had a bunch of girl-buddies in college, including my college roommate, Claire. I didn't like her that much, because she thought I was a bit of a slut, and I thought she was a bit too masculine. I've always been a tomboy, and so was she. I think we might have been a bit competitive. She introduced me to Tom as a blind date. Tom was so sweet. He looked me in the eye instead of the boobs, he loved my hair and my jewelry, and even liked to see me in pants. I had a pair of red pants that drove him crazy. He was so polite and so nice. I was so sick of jocks, zoomies, and frat-boys. Tom was special. He's more of a girl than I am."

Conversion

Lois was shocked "So he doesn't mind that Russ is so girlie?"

Ann shook her head, "No, he doesn't like it at all. He is so worried that Russ will be bullied, picked on, or worse if anybody finds out. We have to keep it a secret."

Lois nodded. "I was so terrified that Buddy would find out. Lloyd is a good man, but he is a bit macho. He adores Steve, who is a jock and loves sports and does well. Mark has been a disappointment. Steve caught Mark wearing a dress and couldn't wait to tell Lloyd. Lloyd gave Mark 20 lashes with the belt."

Anne winced. "Ouch, I remember how bad it hurt when I had five lashes. I can't even imagine 20. Pop hurt me so bad once that Ma took me out to the woodshed herself. She'd strap me a few times, then she would hit an old saddle, while I screamed like I was dying. Thank God that pop never wanted to see the marks. Since I had polio that almost killed me, and had to go through painful treatment to recover, I think he figured I had been punished enough."

Lois was about to cry. "I don't know what I'm going to do! If Lloyd hits Mark again, the doctor will call child protection. I've never seen him that violent with Steve. It's like he hates Mark."

Anne shook her head. "Keeping it a secret isn't much better. The boys at school seem to pick up on it, and I can't tell you how many times Russ has come home sobbing, telling me how much he hates being a boy. He gets asthma, and when he goes to the hospital, they get so suspicious about all the bruises. He's been in the hospital 8 weeks this year alone."

Lois shuddered. "I've been there. Lloyd took Mark to one of Steve's soccer practices. The juniors coach put Mark on the field. He ended up in the hospital for three weeks. It was horrible."

Conversion

Anne smiled. "It's so nice to know I'm not alone. I don't know what to do. I'm terrified that Pop will find out. I don't know what I'll do if that happens. Pop has already threatened to send him to a Christian Boarding school because of my smoking. If Russ had to spend his whole life with a bunch of bullying boys, he would be dead in a month."

Lois smiled. "Pop wants to send Mark to camp. Some Christian Summer camp called IdRaHaJe."

Anne smiled. "I'd Rather Have Jesus", Will went there when he was acting up when he was 8. He ended up getting saved. Not sure if it really took though. Russ knows his Bible too well. He sometimes gets into Biblical discussions with Grandpa that even I can't follow. Pop loves it though."

Lois laughed quietly, "Yes, Mark has been reading his Bible almost since he first learned to read. Sometimes I get the impression that he's bored with school, other times I think he's terrified."

The Cellar

Tuesday, both Mark and Russ were getting bored. They had read their books, and there wasn't much to do. Russ suddenly smiled. "I have an idea. We have to be quiet, while Grandma and Grandpa are taking their nap. I want to show you something."

Russ led Mark down into the cellar, then went to a drawer, and pulled out a skeleton key. He opened another door at the back of the cellar, unlocking it with the key. Mark followed, and Russ locked the door behind them. "This way no one will walk in on us."

Russ turned on the light. The room was filled with beautiful dresses. "Grandma showed me this place when she caught me snooping through her drawers. These are old prom dresses, bridesmaid dresses, and other dresses she doesn't want Grandpa to know about. She likes to come down here and look at the dresses to bring back happy memories. We can try on anything that is not too small for us."

Soon both of them were in pretty dresses, giggling quietly, pretending to be at a party or a wedding. They tried on a couple of dresses.

Finally, they put their boy clothes back on. Mark hugged Russ, then kissed him on the mouth. Then he pressed his tongue into Russ's mouth, and Russ yielded for a moment. Russ even started to moan.

Russ pulled back. "Mark, I'm so flattered that you find me attractive, and I understand, but you aren't my type. I don't want to kiss you, but I do want to be your friend."

Mark cried, "Thank you for not getting mad, you are wonderful."

Russ held him and hugged him "I know, it's hard sometimes. You know I'll always be your friend."

Conversion

Summer Camp

Mark was excited and terrified. It had been a month since he spent that week with Russ, and now he was going to IdRaHaJe. The thought of having to sleep with a bunch of other boys, not be a girl, and being in a camp with a bunch of Christians scared him. Would they like him? Would they hate him? Would the beat him? Would any of them kiss him?

He walked in and found an empty bunk in the back of the cabin, near the back door. If he had to get out, he could, but he also wouldn't be the center of attention. Another boy came in shortly after and took the bunk above. "I'm James, pleasure to meet you."

Mark smiled, James was rather cute. "I'm Mark, it's a pleasure to meet you."

One of the camp counselors poked her head in, "Come on boys, time to eat, you can get settled in later."

They got to the commissary and were greeted by another counselor. They gave their names. "Your cabin is at table 12, you should sit with them today and get to know each other. Starting tomorrow, you can sit with them or with others."

As they walked to the table, they saw other boys their own age. They were all friendly and polite. It seemed that all these boys were a bit frail and timid. Suddenly a larger boy come to sit with them. "I'm John, I was here last year. Looks like I got stuck with the wimps again."

The others tried to be polite, but John had made them uncomfortable. Just before the evening prayer, another boy came and gave John a big hug.

Conversion

"Ralph, so good to see you, I was worried you wouldn't be here this year."

Ralph huffed, "Yeah, I had to apologize to the staff, but they decided that I needed the redemption, so they want me back for another try. They're hoping I'll get saved this year."

The pastor stood up, made several announcements, and everybody bowed their heads in prayer, everyone but Ralph and John. The prayer went on for 10 minutes, and finally the Preacher said, "In Jesus Name", and the room responded "Amen".

The food was served. Hot dogs, beans, potato salad, and coleslaw. It was like a picnic. Everybody dug in.

After dinner, everybody went back to the cabin. Their counselor had everyone go around and introduce themselves, saying their names and something about themselves. Finally, the leader said "OK, Lights out. Bathrooms are outside, and you can use the door at the front or back of the cabin but be sure to wear your shoes and be quiet."

Mark couldn't believe how dark it was. He looked out the window and it seemed like there were a million little stars out. The moon was a tiny sliver and just coming up on the horizon. Within minutes, Mark was asleep.

The next day, there were so many activities. At breakfast there was a sing-along, there were pancakes, eggs, and bacon, and plenty of everything. There was also juice and milk. Mark could tell that the juice had been watered down. It was probably made from frozen, and they put too much water in it. The eggs were powdered, and the pancakes were Bisquick. Still, the food was healthy and filling.

Afterword, there were various activities. Mark decided to try his hand at leather craft. He sat at a table with several girls. They

were using tools to make patterns. The counselor asked what he wanted to make. He decided that he would try making a small purse for his mom. The other girls showed him how to trace the pattern with a tool, then how to use various stamps and a wooden mallet to add details. Mark spent the rest of the afternoon with the girls, talking and working. He had created an exquisite pattern and the other girls were quite impressed. Then they showed him how to put it all together using leather thong, like shoelaces made out of leather. When he was done, he had a beautiful purse.

After that, the girls invited him to sing with them. They went to the chapel and there was a small choir of mostly girls and a few boys. The teacher started to lead the class in a simple song, Go Tell it On the Mountain. Mark knew the song and started singing the descant he sang with his mother. The music teacher noticed and asked Mark what he was doing.

Mark smiled. "My mom taught me how to sing the descant, we like to sing it during the church hymn."

The director asked Mark to come to the microphone and sing the descant so the other girls could learn it. He pointed to a few of the soprano girls "When you pick it up, you can join in, OK?"

The group started singing again, and Mark sang the descant. His high light soprano voice carried across the room. By the second verse, two other girls had stepped up to join him, and by the third verse, another girl had joined in. The sound was quite beautiful and all of the girls singing descant were on pitch and in rhythm.

They started another song, which Mark knew, and he again sang a descant. Again, the other girls picked it up quickly, and were joining in.

The director was delighted. "I want you four to sing the descant in front when we sing this at dinner tonight, OK. You all have such

lovely soprano voices. The rest of you will also sing in front, to lead the singing, OK?"

One of the girls singing melody said, "It's like we're doing a concert!"

Everybody got excited. The went through a few more songs, and the director had them singing in two-part harmony. Mark sang Alto for another song, and again had a strong voice. He was again asked to sing into the microphone so the other altos could hear the part better. Soon the whole choir was singing in beautiful harmony, all of the voices strong and confident.

At dinner, right after the pastor said the blessing, he invited the choir to come up and sing. Mark and the other four girls came to the microphone, and the rest of the choir fell in behind. They started singing, and soon the entire room was singing the old favorite. The words were projected onto a screen above them, with slides changing to show the words.

When they split for the final song, Mark and another Alto took one mic, and two sopranos took the other, the choir behind them joined in to create a beautiful harmony. Mark's voice was strong and confident. He had been singing in front of his church since he was 5, and he loved to sing. He often sang into a mic, even when it was as part of a choir. At the end, the room applauded.

The director came forward. "Would you like to hear more of that this week?"

The room broke out in thunderous applause. The whole choir was elated, they were so happy that everybody enjoyed the music.

After dinner, everyone turned in to their cabins. Mark was chatting with the girls and got in later than the rest.

Conversion

John and Ralph blocked the door. "This is a BOY'S Cabin, we don't let GIRLS sleep here."

Mark smiled. "Well, I don't think I could sleep with the girls either. Wouldn't YOU like to though?"

The boys in the cabin started to giggle.

John smiled. "I don't think you're really a boy, Prove it"

Ralph nodded. "Yeah, prove it, drop your pants!"

John started leading the boys it a chant "Prove it! Prove it! Prove it!"

Suddenly John and Ralph grabbed his arms and shoved him down backwards onto the nearest bed. Two of the larger boys pulled down his pants, but the jockey shorts were still on. Within a minute, all of the boys were standing in a circle, waiting for the big reveal. Finally, they pulled down the shorts. They were all stunned.

"Oh my God, it's so tiny, it's barely more than a bump"

"He doesn't have any nuts, there's nothing there!"

"He's a freak, no wonder he's so girly!"

Suddenly they heard a whistle blow. It was the counselor. The boys jumped away, standing at attention. Mark just lay on the bed, sobbing, unable to move. He was terrified.
The counselor yelled as loud as he could, "EVERYBODY IN YOUR BEDS! NOW!!!"

Mark just lay there sobbing, "I'm so sorry!"

Conversion

The counselor sat down next to him. "It's OK, pull up your pants and come with me. We need to talk." Mark got dressed, but he was still crying. He couldn't stop. Finally, he hugged the counselor, still crying.

The counselor walked him out of the cabin. A counselor from the next cabin heard the commotion and came out. "I'm going to take this one up to see the pastor. The boys got a bit rough with him. See if you can figure out who set this up!"

It didn't take long for John and Ralph to fess up. In fact, they were quite proud of themselves for exposing the "Sissy Freak".

Pastor Tom was still in his study, enjoying a nice warm fire when the counselor knocked, holding a shivering and terrified Mark against him. It was a warm night, but Mark was shaking with terror.

Pastor Tom grinned at the young counselor. "Leave him with me. Get back to your cabin and get this all sorted out." Pastor Tom led Mark over to the fire. "So, tell me what this is all about!"

Mark was crying. "I got to the cabin and Ralph and John wouldn't let me in. They thought I was a girl, next thing I know, they are shoving me onto the nearest bed and pulling down my pants. I couldn't move. Then they pulled down my underwear. They called me a freak!"

Pastor Tom smiled. "It couldn't be that bad! You might be a little small, but not a freak. Why don't you let me take a look?"

Mark cowered in terror, he stood up to run, but the pastor was quick and strong. "DROP YOUR PANTS BOY! SHOW ME WHAT'S SO TERRIBLE!"

Conversion

Mark was sobbing as he pulled down his pants and his underwear. He was terrified! He wanted to run but the Pastor held him fast, his thumbs digging into his shoulders.

Pastor couldn't believe his eyes "Oh my, that is unusual isn't it? I've never seen anything like it!"

He sat back down, holding Mark tightly by one wrist. "Let me touch it for a minute. I won't hurt you."

He began to feel around what should have been a scrotum. There was nothing there. He pressed his little finger into the inguinal canal, there was nothing. It was like there was no testicles anywhere. "Lay down on the couch boy, I need to look closer." He pulled out a flashlight, he examined the missing scrotum. He saw a zig-zagged line. It was a scar, like he had been sewn shut years ago. "What's your name, boy?"

Mark sniffled. "Mark Woodward, sir."

Pastor Tom stiffened. "You're Woody's grandson? Earnest Woodward?"

Mark nodded. "Yes, he's my grandfather."

Pastor Tom smiled. "Well, at least they know you're not a girl now, don't they?"

Mark looked so sad. "Yes sir, I guess I'm a boy!"

Pastor Tom stopped short. "You GUESS you're a boy?"

Mark nodded. "Sometimes I wonder."

"What do you MEAN you WONDER?"

Conversion

Mark was scared again. "I'm sorry sir, I mean some kids are born with flippers for arms, or a cleft palate, or with Downs Syndrome. Maybe I have a birth defect, like I'm a girl inside and the little thing down there is just a birth defect."

Pastor Tom started to get angry. "Are you trying to tell me you think you're a girl?"

Mark cowered. "I'm just saying I might have been better off if I had been a girl!" He started to cry again.

Pastor Tom tried to calm himself. "Are you saying God made a Mistake?"

Mark shook his head. "No sir, God doesn't make mistakes. A kid born with Downs is different, but it isn't a mistake. He might not be as smart as other kids, but he's the perfect example of unconditional love and forgiveness. I've seen kids with Downs get beat up by a bully, and immediately forgive them. They are perfect examples of Christ's love. Is that a mistake?"

Mark continued, "I'm different. I don't know why, I don't know how different, I don't know what to do about it, but I'm just an example of God's infinite variety in creation. Why did he make me this way? I don't know. I don't think it was God's mistake. It may just be that other people can't accept someone like me, like some people can't accept a child with Downs."

Pastor Tom was stunned. "Well Mark, that's probably the best way of looking at it, but that doesn't make you a girl, though you have a lovely voice. You sounded beautiful in the choir tonight."

Mark smiled. "Thank you sir, I really enjoyed singing with them. I like singing for my church too. Sometimes, in the summer, I sing a solo or duet with one of the older kids. I like making people happy."

Conversion

Pastor Tom smiled. "Careful, pride is a sin. You don't want to get a big ego. Pride cometh before the fall"

Mark smiled. "No sir, when I sing, I'm scared, and I'm worried that I will make mistakes. God gave me a pretty singing voice, and this is a way that I can serve others, but it's scary."

Pastor Tom laughed. "I know the feeling, sometimes, when I'm about to preach, I'm scared too. I'm so nervous I'm shaking. I like to think that it's God, shaking the truth out of me."

Mark laughed lightly. "I like that, I know that feeling".

Pastor Tom patted Mark on the shoulder. "Would you be willing to sing a solo or duet at evening vespers? After my blessing?"

Mark smiled. "If you think it will help you reach the kids, yes sir."

Pastor Tom smiled. "I think it might. Let me walk you back to your cabin. You don't have a flashlight and it's dark outside."

Pastor Tom walked Mark back to the cabin and pulled the counselor aside. "What was the problem, Rick?"

Rick was nervous. "John and Ralph led the attack, sir. I think they need to be assigned to a cabin with the older boys. I was hoping they would help the new boys get settled, but if they are going to be abusive, they can pick on kids their own size."

Pastor Tom shook his head. "Let's not be so hasty. If they promise not to cause any more trouble, they can stay, but I don't want anyone else being hurt or humiliated or I will just send them home."

Conversion

Panty Raid

The rest of the week, Mark spent most of his time with his girl friends. They did crafts in the morning and sang in the afternoon. Mark sang solos 2 nights at the dinner prayer and helped lead the singing around the campfire. Most of the boys in his cabin were nicer to him, and nobody picked on him.

The second week, on Tuesday, John and Ralph got all the boys, including Mark, into a huddle.

John led off. "OK boys, tonight we are going on a panty raid. We are going to run through the girl's cabin and each of us has to bring back one pair of girl's panties."

Ralph followed. "Anyone who doesn't bring a pair back will have to WEAR a pair of the panties."

Mark didn't want to go. These girls were his friends. He didn't want to scare them or hurt them. He even thought he'd be willing to wear the panties, but he realized they would probably try to embarrass him even more than they did that night they attacked him.

Ralph led the charge, and John took up the rear. Mark and Jimmy were the last to enter and had to be pushed in by John. Mark tripped and John ran past him. Mark got up and tried to grab a pair of panties and head for the door, but he couldn't get it open. The boys were holding the door shut. Mark started to run for the back door, but four girls blocked that exit.

The girls grabbed him and held him by his arms. He couldn't move. He had been tricked and now he was trapped. He looked around the room. He knew most of the girls. They did crafts with him or sang with him. There were four girls who were playing softball and soccer with the boys. They scared him.

One of the bigger girls came forward "Since you wanted our panties so badly, you should WEAR them."

Another of the big girls laughed "Why stop at panties, I think you should wear EVERYTHING!"

Mark suddenly stopped struggling. He was caught in a whirlwind of emotions and thoughts. He just froze. Suddenly, he just went calm.

One of the girls pulled out a pair of black satin panties. "Put these on Sissy boy!"

Mark pulled down his pants, and the girls pulled down his jockey shorts.

"Look at it, it's so tiny".

Mark quickly pulled up the panties, and in an instant, the little lump had disappeared completely. The girls were amazed that it appeared to be gone. He was as smooth as they were. Another girl pulled out a black satin bra and handed it to Mark. Mark hesitated, then took it, fastened it behind his back, and put his arms through the straps.

The girls cheered, impressed "Wow, I've had boys snap my bra and unhook it, but I've never seen a guy who could put one on so easily." Another girl pulled out a dark blue summer dress.

Mark smiled. "I look better in Red, but I'll try this one." Suddenly the girls were all laughing. Mark smiled as he pulled on the dress and let it fall down, pulling it down to his waist, and letting the hem fall to just above his knees.

Conversion

Suddenly, the girls stopped laughing. They were shocked to see a pretty girl with short hair. One of the tomboys opened a drawer and pulled out an Auburn wig. "My mom made me wear this when they brought me. I had cut off my own hair and it looked terrible, at least that's what MOM said. I'd get a crew cut if I could."

Mark took the wig, leaned forward, put it the right way, and set the clips, then he straightened up, flipping the hair up and over, to create the look of a nice full mane. One of the girls handed him a brush. He went to the mirror and brushed out his hair. In less than a minute, the soft gentle waves of the wig were tamed. He turned to face his would-be tormentors.

Almost in unison, the girls said "Wow, that's amazing, he's so pretty." Nobody could believe it.

Another girl he didn't know pulled out a pair of high strappy sandals. Mark slid them onto his feet, quite surprised that they not only fit, they were a size too large. He began to walk across the room, and then back.

The whole cabin of girls cheered, they were so excited. Mark was actually beautiful. Suddenly they were all hugging him and laughing with him, telling him how pretty he looked. One of the girls started putting on some make-up, and another plucked his eyebrows. Then they put on some mascara on, and some lipstick. Then a brush to add some blush. They all stepped back to see, and he walked down the hall and back. Everybody ooh'd and ah'd.

"She's beautiful"

"She's the prettiest girl in the cabin"

Suddenly the boys started knocking at the door, "Let us see the little fairy, send him out!"

Conversion

One of the big girls opened the front door, and let the boys in. The boy's filed in, expecting to see an ugly boy in a dress, looking ridiculous. Instead, they saw an amazingly beautiful young lady, better that the prettiest girls at their schools. The girls giggled as the boys stood there stunned.

"Who is SHE?"

"Wow, she's a hottie!"

"She's a babe!"

Mark smiled, waved and said, "Hi guys!"

Suddenly the boys realized who it was. "Mark, is that really you?"

Mark couldn't resist the urge to flirt. "I'm Marcia, how are you tonight?"

Suddenly all of the boys were silent. All that teasing, yet all they could see was this beautiful girl who called herself Marcia.

Marcia walked up to John and waved a finger to one of the big tough tomboys. "John, I think I have the perfect girl for you, but I'm afraid she might beat the crap out of you."

The girls started to giggle.

Marcia sidled up to Ralph and pressed herself against him. "Is that a banana in your pocket or are you just glad to see me? Feels more like a gherkin."

The girls all giggled, Ralph tried to step out without completely tenting his shorts.

Conversion

Then the boys and the girls started praising Marcia. She glowed, so happy to be accepted by both the boys and the girls.

One of the girls called out "Marcia, sing for us, we'll back you up."

Marcia started into the verse of "You Light up my Life". In seconds, the girls had found a harmony to back her up. Soon the whole cabin was singing the chorus, and those who could sing were backing her on the verses.

They were all still clapping when the counselors walked in, both the girls' counselor and the boys' counselor, and then, to everyone's horror, especially Marcia's, Pastor Tom walked in.

Pastor Tom was livid. "What are all you children doing up, out of bed, singing in the middle of the night. You should all be in bed, sleeping." He looked around, then he saw the one girl, totally out of place. Everyone else was in bed clothes, and camp gear, and then there was this beautiful girl in a frilly dress and strappy heels. "You there, what are you doing dressed like some kind of tart?"

One of the girls came forward. "Please sir, we asked Marcia to sing for us, and she did. She has a beautiful voice. We dressed her up this way. It's not her fault."

Suddenly the boys' counselor recognized who Marcia really was. "Mark, why are you dressed like a girl!?!"

One of the big girls nodded. "We made him dress up for us Pastor Tom. The boys did a panty raid and we caught Mark, and we made him dress up like a girl. Didn't think he'd turn out so pretty. He seems to like it too. He didn't put up much of a fight."

Pastor Tom had had enough. "Girls, back into bed, boys, back to your cabin and into bed. You MARCIA are coming with me." He

Conversion

grabbed Mark by the ear and held him out at arm's length, like he was a piece of rancid meat.

Pastor Tom marched Mark all the way back to his cabin. Mark tripped a few times in the heels, but Pastor Tom was more surprised at how well he walked in the ridiculous heels. Obviously, this wasn't the first time.

Tom pushed Mark into his bedroom and bent him over the foot of the bed. "Don't move Marcia!" He went to the side of his bed and pulled out a bamboo cane, about four feet long, half inch diameter, and swung it. It whistled as it slashed through the air.

Pastor Tom pulled up the dress and yanked down the panties. "I obviously can't put you with the boys, because you are obviously not a boy, and I can't put you with the girls because you are obviously not a girl. I'm going to give you a caning while I think about what to do with you."

Mark laced his fingers together so he wouldn't be tempted to reach back. He knew that would only make things worse. The first blow came down hard and fast across his buttocks. Mark wanted to scream, but he didn't want to give this sadistic bastard the satisfaction of a scream on the first blow. The second blow came down hard and fast across the mid-thighs. Mark wanted to kick or convulse, but he held completely still. He was already starting to cry. The third blow came down across the small of his back. It was too much, and Mark let out a wail.

Pastor Tom gave a sadistic leer, he was enjoying this immensely. He had this vulnerable little sissy, and she was so delightfully submissive, but he didn't want this thing to enjoy it. "That's right! You sissy trollop, I'm going to whip you so hard you will scream for mercy. Let me hear you scream." The next blow came exactly where the first had landed, and the skin began to bleed. Mark screamed a high-pitched wail.

Conversion

Pastor Tom pulled off the other sandal. "Best if we make them match". He delivered two blows to the other foot as he held it still.

Mark couldn't believe the pain. It was so intense. He suddenly threw up all over the bed, then he heaved some more.

Pastor Tom was furious. "Look at what you did to my bed. Just for that...", he grabbed the other foot and gave her two more.

Mark heaved again, giving up whatever was left of breakfast, lunch, and dinner.

Pastor Tom wanted to kill this creature. It was temptation and loathing incarnate in one body. "I obviously can't put you with the boys, or the girls, and you just threw up all over my bed, so I guess I just have to put you with the animals."

He threw the lump of whimpering flesh over his shoulder like a sack of flour. All the fight was gone. He took her out to a metal shed at the edge of a field. He pulled out the feed that had been stored in there, until there was nothing but bare floor. It was made of corrugated steel, only 3 feet high, 4 feet long, and 2 feet wide. Too short to stand up in, too short to lie down in, and barely room to sit up in.

"Maybe a few days in the box will make you see reason. It gets very cold at night and gets sweltering hot during the daytime. No windows and it's far enough away, no one will hear your calls for help. You are going to be a boy, whether you like it or not. You're an abomination, and you should be destroyed, but I'll try to save your soul before you die."

That night Mark shivered through the night, passing out from the cold. The next morning, he was dehydrated and had given up caring. By noon, he had passed out from the heat. The second night, he barely woke up at all. Dehydrated and malnourished,

having puked up what little he had, he was slipping away. He had all but given up. The third day, he was delusional. He thought he was back in heaven again. He was ready to give up, but he was told to go back. The fourth day, he heard someone walking toward him. He heard the door being opened. Suddenly he felt an arm dragging him out of the box. It was Pastor Tom.

"Get this THING, this ABOMINATION, this DEMON FROM HELL, OUT OF MY CAMP before I kill her myself."

After so many days of darkness, he couldn't see. Then he heard his father's voice. "Do I need to strap you again, Mark?". Mark lifted his dress. He didn't care who saw, the welts had broken open, and become infected.

Then he heard his mother's voice. "Oh my GOD! What have you DONE! You sadistic BASTARD!" She pulled her son into her. "It's OK honey, we're going home".
Pastor Tom took chances, he had to stay in control of this situation. "If you tell a soul, I'll make sure you never see ANY of your children again. My congregation includes social workers, all I have to do is tell them how you indulged this little pervert, giving him to the devil. They will take care of the rest.

Mark didn't even react, he could barely move. Lloyd had to throw him over his shoulder to carry him to the car. He put Mark in the back of the station wagon, because it was the only way Mark could avoid laying on the blisters that were festering.

Mark slept the whole way home. His parents didn't realize that he was suffering from dehydration and malnutrition. He hadn't had water in almost three days and hadn't had food in four. In addition, the infected welts were causing a fever, and the cold and heat had pretty much driven him to the brink. By the time he got home, he had passed out and they couldn't wake him up.

Conversion

Finally, the next morning, Lois forced him to wake up enough to take some chicken broth. Just enough so he could keep it down and he would retain the water.

Turning Point

Mark spent the next week in bed. He didn't want to eat or drink. He didn't want to do anything but sleep. He knew he should be doing house-work, but he couldn't bring himself to do anything Marcia liked. He felt like a shell. An empty husk.

One night, he got up, while his parents were asleep. He pulled out a bottle of aspirin and took it to his room. At first, he wanted it for the pain, so he took four. An hour later, he took four more, an hour after that he took four more. He continued through the night, taking four every hour. He finally fell asleep in the morning.

Lois came in after work to check up on him. He was sleeping but hadn't stirred. His bed smelled of urine. She began to worry. She shook him to wake him up. He tried to sit up and just fell over. Lois try to sit him up again, and this time he just fell onto the floor like a wet dish rag. Lois shook him to wake him up. "What's wrong with you, Mark?".

Mark mumbled, "Took some Aspirin."

Lois looked at the bottle. It was almost empty, but it had been full the night before. She shook him. "How many did you take Mark?"

Mark held up 4 fingers.

Lois called Lloyd at work. "I need to take Mark to the doctor right now. I think he took too many aspirin."

Lloyd was worried. "Keep him awake. Try to keep him sitting up."

Lois tried to wake Mark again. He's started to wretch. He brought up blood. Lois called the doctor. The doctor was adamant. "Don't waste time, take him directly to the Emergency Room".

Conversion

When Lloyd got home, he picked up his son over his shoulder and took him down to the station wagon. He wasn't even moving. Lois gave him a pot in case he needed to vomit again. They drove directly to the emergency room and pulled up at the door. Lloyd got out of the car and pulled the boy out of the back. "He's throwing up blood."

Mark had passed out again. He had been wearing a nightgown because his welts hurt too bad to wear even Pajamas. Lois was dreading this visit. It could mean losing her son.

In the examining room, doctor lifted the nightgown and gasped in horror. The welts were deep and festering. The heartbeat was thready and irregular dipping below 40 bpm, the blood pressure was too low as well, 90/60, and the fever was up to 104. They started an IV. Mark threw up again. The pan was filled with blood.

The doctor tried to rouse Mark. "Mark, did your father do this to you, did he give you these welts?"

Mark shook his head. "No, Pastor Tom".

The doctor was confused. "Stay with me Mark, who is Pastor Tom!"

Mark was groggy. "Summer camp. IdRaHaJe. I'd Rather Have Jesus"

The doctor needed to know more. "Did you try to kill yourself last night?"

Mark nodded. "I hurt so I took aspirin. Four every hour."

The doctor stepped back "OK Mark, just rest now."

Mark nodded and fell asleep.

Conversion

The doctor came out to the waiting room.

"This is your fourth visit to the Emergency room in 3 months. I need to know one thing. What is Camp Idrahaje?"

Lloyd nodded. "Camp I'd Rather Have Jesus, we sent him there in hopes that he would straighten out. That didn't work out very well. My pop thought it would help Mark get over this idea of being Marcia."

Lois fumed. "Yeah, that worked out REAL WELL! Pastor Tom caned him and locked him in a hot-box for four days in a row!"

The doctor heard what he needed. "Mr. Woodward, you are a danger to your child. I have a good mind to report you to child protection. This boy is becoming a regular visitor."

Lloyd was contrite. "I'm sorry Doctor, you're right. I just don't know what to do. Mark almost insists on being Marcia, even when he knows he's going to get a beating for it."

The doctor nodded. "OK, first I have to get him stable, so we have to admit him. Second, he admitted to me that this wasn't an accident. He tried to kill himself. As a result, once he's stable, we have to keep him for a 72-hour Psychiatric evaluation."

Lloyd chortled. "Yes, any boy who wants to be a girl, MUST be crazy. Especially when he knows he's going to get a beating for it." The pure anger on Lois' face told him he had better just shut up.

Conversion

Evaluation

It took over a week to get Mark stable. They couldn't pump his stomach because he staggered the doses. The bleeding in his stomach and intestines couldn't be stopped surgically, and the electrolytes were way off.

The psychologist had come to see him three times already. Mark told him about how he had read about how to commit suicide in an army manual, and how he had planned his attempt carefully. He knew how to stagger the medications rather than taking them all at once, so it wouldn't just come up in vomit, and so they couldn't just pump out his stomach.

But when the doctor asked him WHY he did it, he only said one word, "Marcia."

When Lois came to visit, the psychologist asked Lois about Marcia. Lois told him everything, how she had caught Marcia, and how she had given Mark all of the housework, and how quickly she adapted, getting very good at it and liking it.

Then she talked about how Steve had discovered Marcia, told Lloyd, and how Lloyd had belted him.

Then she told what she knew of the summer camp. How he had dressed as a girl and how the sadistic Pastor Tom had caned him and stuck him in the hot-box.

Lois was frantic to get him some help but didn't know where to turn. She even related how their own Pastor had talked to Mark, just before he locked himself in a sealed hot car for three hours.

Lois and the therapist met with Mark when he was well enough. The therapist was kind and gentle. "Mark, we need to keep you for three more days, to evaluate you. We will move you to the

psychiatric ward, and you will be observed and evaluated there to determine the best way to treat you."

Mark looked into her eyes, "Are you going to lock me up?"

The therapist didn't dare lie. "We'd rather you agree voluntarily, but if necessary, yes, we can force you and you will be locked up, all we really need is your mom's signature. The evaluation is to decide the best way to treat you. I hope we won't have to lock you up long term."

Mark nodded "Fine, I do need help, so I agree, where do I sign? Mom can sign too."

Minutes after they signed the papers, his mother left. He was led to a different part of the hospital. The therapist opened the door and led him in, then she made a point of checking the door, showing that it was locked, and he would not be able to leave until they decided he could. Voluntary or not, Mark was locked in.

Somehow, Mark felt safer, now that he was locked in. He hoped that they would not try to kill Marcia again. He began to have hope. He trusted that because he was in a hospital, he would be safe, they would help him.

They led him to the common room. There were several other people his own age, and they were joking and laughing. He was told to join them.

Mark sat between two girls, across from the boys. One of the girls introduced herself "I'm Sarah, this is Jill, and this is Lily. What are you in for?"

Mark smiled. "One of my best friends is named Lily, and the other one is Sarah. It's good to meet you? What do you mean what am I in for? I'm here for observation?"

Conversion

Sarah laughed. "You can tell us. Suicide? Hitting someone? Drug addiction?"

Mark understood. "Oh, that! Suicide."

Sarah smiled. "Oh yeah? Me too! So is Jill! How'd you do it?"

Mark smiled. "It was pretty dumb. I took 4 aspirin every hour so they wouldn't be able to pump my stomach."

Jill laughed. "Yeah, I tried to take them all at once. I threw up, and the rest they got with the stomach pump. I hate that charcoal."

Sarah held out her wrists. "I tried to slit my wrists", that didn't work out well at all."

Mark smiled. "You shouldn't cut across like that, you could cut a tendon, and you won't get any arteries." He felt her pulse. "There, where you feel your pulse, you take the knife straight down, then give it a twist. You should bleed out in a few minutes."

Sarah thought a minute, then asked, "But doesn't that hurt going so deep? And what if you miss?"

Mark smiled. "If you want to make sure you don't miss, put on a pair of sunglasses or glasses, then take the razor blades across the temples. For quick and painless, go for the carotid artery. He felt his pulse. "There, you can feel it in your neck. I guess it's a bit like a needle rush."

A therapist walked over. "Mark, follow me."

She led him to the quiet room. "Since you can't keep quiet about the ways to commit suicide, I'm putting you into the quiet room for a while. Keep in mind that the people who were listening have

already attempted suicide, and might try one of your ideas, and end up dead. Is that what you want?"

Mark shook his head. "Oh, NO, you're right, I hadn't thought of that. You're right. I'll go in now, but I promise to be good when I come out."

Mark walked into the center of the room and waited for the door to close. There was the smell of urine, Lysol, and bleach. It wasn't the most pleasant smell, but he knew he would get used to it in a few minutes. The walls were padded, so he leaned up against one of them. Then he sat and started to sing one of his songs. Since this was a quiet room, he could sing as loud as he wanted, and nobody would hear him. He had been singing happy fun songs for almost two hours, when the door opened.

The therapist lifted him up. "You are having way too much fun in here! Get out. I want you to go sit on the couch and not say a word, OK?"

When he sat down, the girls were still talking. When they asked him a question, he mimed zipping his mouth shut. Sarah laughed. "Oh, you aren't allowed to talk?"

Mark nodded.

Jill giggled, "OK, but we're going to try to make you laugh!"

For the next hour, they told silly jokes, and Mark giggled and laughed, but he never said a word.

Finally, the therapist came over "Bed time everybody, head for your rooms."

The therapist led Mark to his room and showed him the bedroom. "We'll have breakfast at 7:30 AM, sleep well."

Conversion

Mark waited for the door to shut and then checked the door. He was locked in, just as he suspected. He went over to his bed and laid down. He felt at peace, safe, calm. He laid on his back, closed his eyes, and took about 10 deep breaths, and he was asleep.

The next morning, someone opened the door. Mark was awake and had cleaned up as best he could. He had looked to see if there was a camera in the room. He didn't care, but he wondered what they were looking at. He spotted the small camera barely visible through a small hole and waved at it.

He went to breakfast, which was eggs, toast, and bacon. He had a few bites of the eggs, added some salt, and then crunched up some of the bacon into the eggs. He also had some juice.

There was a group session after breakfast, then a few psychological tests before lunch.

After lunch there was a private session with two therapists. It looked like "Good cop, Bad cop".

Good cop was friendly. "Mark, we want to know more about your suicide attempt, what can you tell us?"

Mark proceeded to explain how he had planned it, the many options he considered, and how he was able to carry out the plan. He had been contemplating suicide since his father had belted him. He had researched many different methods and decided to do something that would look like an accident, in case it failed.

Bad cop pressed. "You're telling us WHAT you did, but how did you FEEL about it."

Mark took a deep breath. He explained how, after his beating by Pastor Tom, he had just stopped caring anymore. He was numb. "I

didn't even care whether the suicide attempt succeeded or failed, I just wanted the pain to go away."

Good cop was kind. "What pain, the pain of the caning? The pain of your father's beatings? The pain of being beat up on the soccer field?"

Mark sighed, "That was part of it. There was physical pain. If I overdosed, they would think that I just accidentally took too much for the pain."

Bad cop pressed hard. "But it goes deeper than that doesn't it? It's about Marcia, isn't it?"

Mark started to cry. "They KILLED Marcia!"

Bad cop rubbed his eyes, "But Marcia didn't exist! She wasn't real! She was just some stupid dress-up game you played with the girls next door! Marcia wasn't killed, because Marcia never existed!"

Mark finally got angry for the first time. "Listen you JERK, it's MARK who isn't real, I just pretend to be a boy, so I don't get beat up by the boys at school, so I don't get the belt from my dad, so I don't have something really terrible happen to me, like Pastor Tom, or even worse."

Good cop could see the authenticity coming out. "What could be worse than all those beatings?"

Mark almost bawled. "If I can never be Marcia again! I'd rather be DEAD!!"

Bad cop shook his head "You're a lying piece of shit. You KNOW you are a boy! You KNOW you have a penis! You KNOW that you are not a girl! You ARE a BOY! You MUST accept that!"

Conversion

Mark went calm. "If you say so." Suddenly Mark was cold, unresponsive, almost ignoring the questions. His answers were emotionless, like he was staring off into space and barely paying attention to the conversation. He had shut them out and they knew it.

They took him into a room with several other boys his age. He didn't know any of them. They were talking about sports, girls, sex. They were crude and lewd. Mark wasn't even there. One of them jostled Mark. "Jill has amazing tits, doesn't she? I'd love to get my hands on those puppies."

Mark was suddenly disgusted. "She also has beautiful blue eyes, soft waves in her Auburn hair, and I love the blouse she's wearing today. She's wearing a padded push-up bra, so you idiots are getting all hot and bothered about foam rubber." He got up and walked over to the piano in the corner of the room.

He started to play chords, and sing "You light up my life." Then he stopped. Sam, one of the nicer and cuter boys, came over "That's beautiful, why'd you stop?"

Mark spoke in his Marcia voice, "The last time I sang that song, I was taken away, beaten with a bamboo cane, and locked into a steel box where I nearly froze to death at night, and cooked to death in the afternoon. For three days"

He went to a corner chair and just closed his eyes. He was surprised when he opened them, to see Sam sitting next to him.

Sam had a sad face. "When my parents found out that I was gay, they sent me off to some horrible place. I got locked up and was beaten with belts and canes until I promised never to do it again."

Mark looked up at Sam. "Did you keep that promise?"

Conversion

Sam laughed. "Heck no, but it got me out of that terrible place! You're kind of cute!"

Mark smiled. "Thank you! You should see me in a dress! And you're cute too."

Sam blew him a kiss. "Bye sweetie".

Mark gave a finger wave. "Bye."

Mark started to go back to his room, but almost as soon as he got there, a therapist came in and took him to a room with a bunch of girls.

Mark walked right in and found a seat between a couple of the girls.

Jill laughed. "Hey Mark, good to see you again. We were trying to decide who is cuter David Cassidy or Clint Eastwood?"

Mark giggled. "That's silly, David Cassidy has the dreamiest eyes. You could get lost in them forever."

Sarah giggled. "I win, pay up! I like your hair by the way!"

Mark smiled. "Thank you, I wash with head and shoulders, and condition with Prell. That's such a pretty top Sara, I love the peasant collar on you. It really frames your face nicely."

In a flash they were talking about fashion, make-up, hair, boys, and even sex. One of the girls started talking about her cramps.

Mark asked, "Do you have any Midol?"

Jill smiled. "You know about Midol?"

Conversion

Mark nodded. "Of course. My friend Judy started having periods this summer, and she swears by Midol."

Sarah was laughing hysterically. "Do you have a tampon I can borrow?"

Mark snapped his fingers. "Damn, I left them in my other purse." Suddenly Mark started crying.

Sarah came over and hugged him. "What's the matter Mark, why are you so upset?"

Mark cried. "I made my mom a purse. I was going to give it to her, but they locked me up in that horrible box and I wanted out so bad I forgot everything, including the purse!" He kept crying.

Sarah hugged him again "What happened?"

Mark was crying too hard to speak. "He beat me", and he lifted his shirt. The bruises and welts were still there.

Sarah lifted his shirt even higher. She could see the welts up to his shoulders. "Wow, that's some sick shit".

Jill lifted her shirt to show the bruise on her abdomen. "My dad did this to me!"

Louise turned her back and showed her scars. "My dad beat me with a belt for kissing a boy."

Mark nodded. "My dad belted me last month because my brother caught me in a dress. I got 20 lashes. It was weird though, after about the eighth one, I just went away. Like I wasn't even there anymore."

Sarah nodded. "Dissociating, that's what my therapist called it. I did it when my father was raping me. He'd stick that disgusting thing in me, and I'd just go away."

Mark was crying. "Why are men so mean and nasty? What did we do that was so terrible?"

Louise rubbed his back gently "Nothing honey, some people just think of us girls as punching bags or whipping posts. I swear, I think they get off on watching us scream and cry."

In the other room, the therapists were watching the interaction. Good cop was awed "He just told those girls more about himself in 20 minutes than we could get out of him in all four ER visits, and our most intense interrogation techniques."

Bad cop was stunned "I don't know how this is possible, but I think maybe Mark really IS Marcia inside. He didn't respond to the boys at all, even pulled away. Yet with the girls he was almost immediately at home and comfortable. He trusted them and was ready to speak his true feelings."

The psychologist, who was their supervisor, shook his head "This isn't good. He may be a girl inside, but it's a psychosis. He's losing touch with reality. The treatment for Gender Identity Disorder is extreme. He's right, we have to kill Marcia."

Bad cop looked over "Are you sure? Look how happy SHE is. Clearly that's Marcia, and she has the social skills, the confidence, and the self-esteem. The boy, Mark, is more like a mask, an empty shell. He is hiding, avoiding. About the only boy he interacted with at all, is Sam, and even then, he mentioned the dress, so that may have been Marcia."

Conversion

The psychologist shook his head "You're right, but we have to follow standards of care, and the rules are very strict on this matter."

That night, Mark slept well again. He was almost happy he had come. He only had one more day of evaluation. "I hope they can help me be Marcia!"

The next day was full and busy. After breakfast, the group therapy got very interesting. The girls shared some of those hurts with the larger group. A couple of the guys joked about it, but the others were deeply touched and moved. They had only been looking at these girls as breasts and asses, but suddenly, they were able to see the scars and welts. Four of the boys showed their scars and bruises as well. Marcia had opened up some deep-seated feelings and shared her own. Something magical had happened.

After lunch, there were more tests, and another session with good cop and bad cop. Good cop smiled. "You opened up a LOT last night and this morning. Some real feelings coming out."

Mark smiled. "Yes, being with those girls let me be Marcia. I could be honest and authentic."

Bad Cop barged in. "This stuff about Marcia is bullshit! She's just a part of your personality, she's part of Mark, but you keep hiding behind Marcia."

Mark shook his head. "No, Marcia is the real me, Mark is just a mask, like a costume I put on to hide and protect Marcia. Mark is a miserable little boy who gets beat up because he can't hide the girl well enough to avoid the beatings. Mark doesn't have any friends. He doesn't like people at all."

Good Cop tried to be sympathetic. "But what if you could never be Marcia again?"

Conversion

Mark went cold. "I would rather be DEAD!"

Bad Cop tried to counter. "Come on now, you can't be serious. You're telling me after four trips to the hospital, that you really would rather kill yourself than give up being Marcia? With four failed attempts, it is hard to believe your heart is really in it. It's more like a cry for help. You don't really want to kill yourself, do you!"

Mark smiled, cold as ice. "What makes you think those were my best shots? You saw me the first day. You know I know how to do it, a dozen ways or more. I'd just rather it looks like an accident. My parents are very religious, and I don't want them thinking that I'm in hell because I killed myself".

Bad Cop tried to bluff. "So, you are saying that you actually want to kill yourself?"

Mark shook his head. "No, I said that if I couldn't be Marcia, I would want to kill myself."

Good cop was worried, this was going south fast. "So, what you are saying is that if you are forced to be Mark, to be a boy for the rest of your life, you will end your own life?"

Mark nodded. "That is EXACTLY what I mean!"

Good cop took a deep breath. "I'll just take you to the girl's room then. Let Marcia come out as much as you want. We'll talk later."

Marcia was elated. She had won a small victory. At least now, for the first time, he had made his position crystal clear, in no uncertain terms. The question now was how these people were going to get his father and his brother to accept him as Marcia.

Conversion

Later that evening, a rather large orderly came into the girl's room to pick up Mark.

He made Mark walk in front of him and told him when and where to turn. Mark walked obediently into the office where the psychologist and his parents were already seated. He was told to sit as well. The tall orderly stood over and directly behind him.

The psychologist was blunt. "You said during your evaluation this afternoon, that unless you could be Marcia, that you would end your life, and that you had devices, plans, several ways to do it. Is this correct?"

Mark nodded vigorously. "Yes sir, that is correct."

"Very well, we are going to have to keep you in the hospital, on suicide watch, for a 90-day program of intensive therapy. At the end of this program, you will be free of this delusion that you are a girl, do you understand?"

Mark started to panic. "No, wait, you're going to try to kill Marcia. No, I don't understand, and I won't agree to any treatment that tries to get rid of her."

The psychologist said "That is no longer your decision to make! Since you are a minor, I only need the signatures of both of your parents. I want you to watch as they sign."

Lloyd grabbed the paper and pen and signed with a flourish. "It's about time we ended this Marcia nonsense once and for all."

Lois hesitated. Mark pleaded "Don't do it mom, or I will hate you for the rest of my life. I'm getting out of here now."

As he stood up, he felt the needle in his neck. The orderly had given him a shot, and he was numb, but barely conscious.

Lois shook her head. "I'm sorry Mark, this is for your own good. I should never have let it go this far." Lois signed the paper as well.

The psychologist then said, "I am going to ask that you not make any attempt to contact him for the next two months. He will be fighting this tooth and nail, and any contact in or out could cause a back-slide. We'll call you when it's safe for a visit."

Lois looked into her son's glazed eyes. The Thorazine was kicking in, and he was shaking his head and saying no, but his head was slowly dropping forward. As they left, Mark was out.

Treatment

When Mark came to, he was groggy. He tried to move but he couldn't. He realized that he was in 5-point restraints. His wrists, ankles, and neck were strapped to a gurney so tight he couldn't move.

He heard a voice from behind him. "My name is Dr. Mathews, I'm your psychiatrist. I'll be supervising and administering your treatments for the next three months."

Mark spoke softly. "A pleasure to meet you Doctor Mathews. What did you want to talk about?"

Dr. Mathews leered at the helpless boy. "Oh, my dear boy, you have said quite too much already I'm afraid. You have said that if you could not be Marcia, that you would kill yourself. We have two things we have to do. First, we have to get rid of Marcia. Second, we have to make sure you don't kill yourself. When you leave here, Marcia will be completely gone, quite … dead."

Mark started to struggle, but there was nothing he could do.

"Now you understand, don't you? You won't even MOVE, unless I want you to. I control everything you do for the next 90 days of fun and games. Fun for me anyway. You may not like it so much." The doctor's voice oozed with contempt and glee. It was clear that he enjoyed torturing people.

Suddenly he felt someone sticking something in his mouth. It was like a stick wrapped with cloth.

Then he felt something on his head, like a vice on his temples. Then he felt the most agonizing pain. Every part of his body was cramping, convulsing, He realized that the stick was to keep him from biting his tongue. He couldn't believe the pain. He tried to scream but nothing came out. He struggled against the restraints,

but nothing gave. He felt like he was being stabbed everywhere for what seemed like 90 hours. In reality, it was only 90 seconds.

Then, everything went dark.

As Mark came to, he was dazed and confused. He couldn't remember where he was, what he was doing here, and why he couldn't remember anything about it.

Then he realized that he was bound to a chair. His elbows, wrists, knees, ankles, waist, and neck were all tightly strapped to a lightly padded wooden chair.

He heard a voice from behind. "It's me, Doctor Mathews again. Now for part two of our fun and games. You say you want to be a girl, so I have inserted a metal tube into your rectum, and a wire into your little penis. If you get too excited, you get a shock, like this."

Mark felt a searing shock in his groin. It was horrible. He couldn't imagine that more than a few times.

Dr. Mathews spoke from behind. "You have an IV drip loaded with Epinephrine and Adrenaline. Essentially liquid terror dripping straight into your veins, with no way to stop it. Now, sit back and enjoy the movie, if you can."

The video came up, and there was a beautiful woman, Betty Page, and she looked like she was getting dressed for a party. First, she slid on a pair of lacy panties, then a black satin bra. Just then he felt that excruciating pain from the shock, this one lasted a second or two. The pain and the fear were getting worse. He was feeling a bit nauseous.

Conversion

On the screen, the young lady was putting on a garter belt, and then pulling up one of her stockings. And then another agonizing pulse, this time for about five seconds.

As she pulled up the second stocking, there was a shorter shock, about a second. As the woman put on a short skirt, Mark closed his eyes, hoping to keep from shocked again.

The voice from behind scolded. "If you close your eyes, I will have to tape your eyes open. It's most uncomfortable, so I really don't recommend it. Just be a good boy and keep your eyes open.

He felt another one second jolt, just to let him realize that it didn't matter whether he was aroused or not, he was going to get zapped.

The lady on the screen put on a green satin blouse. She tucked it in and then began doing up the buttons. Jolt.

Then she buttoned her cuffs, and finally she stepped into some lovely peep toe pumps. A jolt of about 10 seconds followed. Mark began to cry.

He suddenly heaved, but nothing came up. Dr. Mathews laughed. "Don't worry, you won't actually bring up anything but maybe some stomach acid. You've been on IVs for two days now, and your stomach has been emptied."

The next film was a slow strip scene, with the girl slowly taking off all of her clothes. The shocking became more frequent and intense, as did the terror and the heaves.

Someone came behind him and turned a knob on the tube above him. "Your blood pressure and heart rate are too high to continue. We don't want you having a heart attack or stroke, so we'll shut off the liquid terror for now."

The next film was just a girl in lingerie dancing. The shocks came frequently. Eventually, Mark passed out.

When he came to, Mark was again strapped to a gurney. Only this time his head was strapped down too.

Dr. Mathews again spoke, unseen. "Next we have a cross between Korean brainwashing and Chinese water torture. Sleep well, if you can."

There was music playing through the speakers. First some annoying country western music. Then some acid rock. Then some pop music. Then some classical. Mark realized that they were probably trying to figure out which annoyed him the most so they could do more of that.

Meanwhile, there was an unpredictable drip of water onto his forehead, every few seconds. The water fell into his eyes, where it collected. Since Mark was unable to move, he couldn't see. The only relief was if he squinted his eyes really tight, and even this only gave a few seconds of respite.

Mark didn't sleep all night long. He was almost looking forward to the shock so he could sleep for a while.

The orderly walked in, saying nothing and wheeled him into the shock room.

Dr. Mathews was again unseen. "Time for day two, only 89 more to go."

Mark opened his mouth for the stick, and then felt the vice on his temples. Suddenly there were those horrible excruciating cramps and convulsions. The pain was so extreme, Mark wanted to die right then and there.

Conversion

Again, he woke up disoriented. He was strapped to the chair again, and he could feel the electrodes. Nobody said a word, but someone turned on the terror juice. He could feel his heartbeat racing already.

The movie opened, this time is was just girls in short skirts and panty-hose and heels, walking down the street, sitting in chairs, standing and talking. Mark wasn't at all aroused, but that didn't stop Dr. Mathews from giving him a good jolt between the legs every few minutes.

The second clip was of a woman stripping slowly. Again, with a jolt every few seconds. The jolts were starting to last longer now and getting more intense.

By the third movie, Mark was heaving again. Nothing to bring up, but still very painful. Finally, the drip was turned off, and again, Mark passed out from the relief.
Of course, it was a short nap as he woke up in the brainwashing chamber again. The drip and the music were getting even more annoying.

By the 5th day, no one had even spoken to him for several days. Even Dr. Mathews had become silent. Did Dr. Mathews take weekends off? Was there any variation in the routine?

By day 9, Mark desperately wanted this to end. He called out, "OK, you win, I surrender."

A voice he didn't know responded. "This is Dr. Daniels. Dr. Mathews is not here today. However, you should know that there is nothing you can do to stop the process. You have 80 more days of this. Please sit back and enjoy the movie." His voice was calm and emotionless.

Conversion

By day 15, Mark was just constantly sobbing. He cried through the movie, he cried through his "nap time" as they called it. He sobbed during his shock therapy.

By day 30, Mark couldn't even remember why he was there. The daily shocks had erased his memories of Pastor Tom, attempting suicide, and being in the hospital.

On day 45, he was having hallucinations. He was having conversations with people during the movies, and yet there was no one there. During "Nap Time" he was seeing things that weren't there. He didn't want to close his eyes, because every time he did, he would see something horrible and terrifying.

On day 50, they let him sleep. There were no more drops on his head. He was still strapped down, though there was no fight left, no sign of struggle. During this time, the music changed too, it was soft relaxing music, but he could hear words like "I enjoy being a boy. I don't want to be a girl", and other subliminal messages. His mind had become like a sponge, he couldn't resist.

On day 60, after his shock, instead of a movie, they gave him a shot. His mind was all jumbled, he couldn't think straight. He hadn't spoken to anyone for weeks, other than the imaginary people of his nightmares.

He was put in a wheelchair, and brought out, into a room with just a couch. A few minutes later, his parents walked in. Mark thought it was another hallucination. At first, he didn't even respond when they talked to him. Tears dripped down his face, but otherwise, there was nothing.

Finally, his mother got up to hug him. He realized there was no tube in his arm, no "juice". He hugged her back like his life depended on it. Then his father came to hug him, Mark barely moved. He just put his arms up and held his head straight.

Conversion

He tried to speak, but he could barely put words together, "Terrible, Torture, Juice, Hungry, Home, Boy."

Suddenly he smiled. He struggled to remember the word he wanted to say. "Marcia!", and then started laughing. He didn't say anything else, he just laughed.

A moment later, someone behind him pushed him through the open door, and back to someplace dark. He felt the needle in his neck again, then everything went black.

Lois watched in horror at the spectacle. "Oh my God, what have they done to my little boy. Lloyd, we need to end this NOW!"

A moment later, the doctor came in to talk to them. "I'm sorry Mr. and Mrs. Woodward that must have been hard to see. Our process is quite simple. We have to try to break down the mind, in this case what Mark called Marcia, and effectively erase it. I won't go into the details, but it's usually quite effective. As you can see, your son has an unusually strong mind, just when we think Marcia is gone, he remembers, and resists. However, he's sufficiently cleared now so we can begin to rebuild the part you want, the boy, so that he will become a man. When we complete the program, he will have lost the desire to become a girl and will be content to be a boy."

Mark was subjected to the most intense portions of the treatment for two more weeks.

Reconstruction

Then one day, after his shock, things were different.

When he woke up, he was in the wheelchair, but he was only strapped down at the wrists and the legs. They showed pictures of girls in pretty lingerie and he immediately felt sick.

The showed him pictures of girls in skirts, and again he heaved. Each picture of a pretty girl made him violently ill. He was unable to look at any of the pretty outfits without getting violently ill.

A voice he couldn't see said, "There are no drugs, just enough D5W to keep him from starving, and he's unable to think about Marcia without being violently ill."

As if on cue, Mark smiled, said "Marcia," and started laughing.

Dr Matthews gave him a jolt that lasted for almost 3 minutes. "Who's laughing now, Funny Man?".

Mark didn't say a word.

That night, they let Mark sleep, but he couldn't. There was no drip, no music, not even a subliminal tape. The silence was deafening. He couldn't sleep at all. He couldn't move, and he didn't try to. He would close his eyes, and terrible visions would go through his head. Visions of girls, and belts, and canes, and shocks, and kicking.

The next morning, they wheeled him into the Shock room. He thrashed his head to say no and refused to open his mouth. Someone held his nose until he had to breathe, and they stuck the stick in his mouth. Then he felt the shock again.

He woke up in a nice soft bed. He wasn't strapped down. There was a nice older man, with white hair, a balding head, and wrinkles in his eyes. He smiled at Mark, and Mark smiled back.

Conversion

"Good morning, Mark. I'm Doctor Murphy. It's time we had a talk."

Mark thought it was a hallucination. Was it a dream? How long before he woke up strapped to the gurney or the chair or the bed for another round if torture and horrors?

"Mark, we need to talk. You need to talk to me."

Mark nodded. "Are you real?"

Dr. Murphy smiled, "Yes, Mark, I am quite real. Do you remember why you are here?"

Mark tried to think, to remember, but he couldn't. There was nothing. "No, I don't."

Dr. Murphy smiled. "That's all right. I'm going to ask you some questions, I want you to answer as quickly as possible. OK?"

Mark nodded. "Hard to think."

"Just do the best you can, OK?"

Mark tried to think. "Ok."

"Mark, what do you think of Soccer?"

Mark winced, squirmed. "I watch soccer. I think."

"Mark, what do you think of mini-skirts"

Mark got violently ill. "Yuck!"

"Mark, what do you think of breasts!"

Conversion

Mark leered "Tits!"

Doctor Murphy smiled, this was a typical male reaction. "Mark, I'm going to show you some photographs, I want you to say whatever comes to your mind."

Mark looked at the first picture, of a pretty girl smiling.

"Nice rack!"

The next picture was of a boy in a football uniform.

"Looks like Steve," and smiled.

The next picture was of three women in a circle, all were wearing short skirts and heels. Mark began to wretch. "Nice asses," and the wrenching began to ease.

Dr. Murphy laughed. "You see Mark, every time you think about wearing girls' clothes, or dressing up as a girl, you get violently ill. If you only focus on having sex with the girl, you don't get so sick."

The doctor showed a picture of a young man in a suit.

Mark smiled. "Mmm, cute!"

Dr. Murphy snapped, "No Mark, not cute, handsome."

Mark nodded. "OK, handsome. VERY handsome."

Dr. Murphy shook his head. "No, he's wearing a nice suit."

Mark smiled, "And he has nice eyes."

Dr. Murphy leaned in. "What do you want to do with him?"

Conversion

Mark smiled. "Talk to him, listen to him, and kiss him."

Dr. Murphy huffed, "No, you want to talk to him, NOT kiss him."

Mark nodded. "Talk, don't kiss. OK."

Mark realized he would do anything to avoid another round of torture. He had no idea how long he had been in, or how long he had left, of if he would ever leave. He had to do what they wanted, say what they wanted, and surrender.

Next came a picture of a soccer player.

"Big, soccer player." He winced. There was a memory, but he couldn't quite remember it.

Then came a picture of his church. "A church."

Dr. Murphy prompted. "A church, you don't remember?"

Mark smiled. "My church."

Dr. Murphy showed him a picture Lily's house.

Mark nodded. "A house, next door."

Dr. Murphy nodded. "What's the last thing you remember?"

Mark smiled. "Starting school. My first day."

Dr. Murphy startled. "Your first day of school ever?"

Mark giggled. "Yes, kindergarten."

Dr. Murphy hesitated. "Do you remember 6th grade?"

Conversion

Mark tried to think. "Oh, I remember 4th grade. Writing cursive!"

Suddenly, Mark tensed up. "Soccer, pain, can't remember."

Dr. Murphy tried to calm him. "It's alright Mark, everything is fine, you're safe now."

One thing Mark knew, for sure, was that he would never be safe here again.

There were no movies that day, and he got to sleep in a real bed with no restraints. Mark realized that there were probably cameras, and any attempt to leave would mean being strapped down again, or worse. He couldn't sleep, so he just closed his eyes and pretended to sleep.

The next morning, a therapist came in. Mark turned and sat up. "Good morning sir."

The therapist smiled. "Get dressed and follow me."

He opened the package the therapist dropped on the bed. It was a pair of boy's pajamas. It was the first time he had worn clothes in a long while. Most of the time, he had just had a cloth gown covering him between torture sessions. When he was dressed, he followed the man into another area. He could hear voices.

The therapist held his shoulders, looked him in the eyes, and shook him once. "Listen, you can't tell anyone about your treatment. If you do, we'll have to start all over again. You don't want that do you?

Mark shook his head vigorously. "No sir, I don't"

The man smiled, "OK, there are two rooms, go talk to anyone you want to, and see if there is anyone you like."

Conversion

Mark walked into the first room, it was full of girls about his age. He didn't know any of them, but he wasn't sure he wanted to either. He stood off to the side. One of the girls was complimenting the other on her outfit. Mark found himself feeling sick. He couldn't even sit down.

He went to the other room. There were boys joking about the girls, talking about their big tits, and great legs. Mark smiled but sat in a chair outside the circle. He didn't talk to anybody, he just listened. He was essentially a fly on the wall.

Finally, he moved a little closer. He laughed when the other boys laughed and nodded as they spoke. He wasn't really listening, it was like their speech was garbled. He just tried to do what the other boys did.

He walked out of the boy's room and went back to the girl's room. He listened for a minute, but just walked out.

He saw the therapist waiting at the door.

"I'm really tired, can I lay down for a while?"

The therapist nodded. "Didn't you sleep well?"

Mark shook his head, "I tried, but I couldn't sleep."

"We can give you something to help you sleep."

They went back to the room with the bed. A few minutes later, the therapist said, "Roll over, this will let you sleep for a few hours." The injection was quick. A few minutes later, Mark was sleeping comfortably.

Conversion

While he was sleeping, the subliminal recordings played. The programming was adjusted to discourage the homosexuality.

Each day, Mark was allowed to enter the two rooms, and each time, he spent most of his time in the boy's room but didn't interact. He would listen and mimic the actions of the other boys.

Release

On the 90th day, Lois and Lloyd came to pick up Mark.

Dr. Murphy led them to an office. "Mark has been through the worst of the treatment, he responded well, but now he is a loner. He is avoiding the girls, but he has no ability to socialize with boys. The situation is precarious at best."

Lloyd huffed, "So what, we need to do another 90 days?"

Lois snapped, "We are NOT putting him through this again. I don't know what you did, but it must have been horrible. There is no way I would agree to put him through that again."

Dr. Murphy held his hand up. "Hold on, Mrs. Woodward, we won't be doing this to him again. However, if he relapses, or he becomes suicidal again, we will have no choice but lobotomy."

Lois shrieked, "LOBOTOMY! HELL NO! You aren't turning my son into some kind of zombie. I won't allow it."

Dr. Murphy held his hand up. "You don't understand. After, this treatment, if there is a relapse, and we don't do the lobotomy, there is very high risk that he will kill himself."

Lois calmed a bit. "You were supposed to CURE him, now it sounds like he's just a time-bomb waiting to go off."

Dr. Murphy nodded. "Your son had extreme Gender Identity Psychosis. He was ready to kill himself if he couldn't be a girl. He was even defiant into the second month. We've programmed him to become violently ill when he thinks about getting dressed, but eventually, in a few years that will wear off, and he could easily revert. Whatever you do, don't remind him that he wanted to be a girl. We've erased his memory of that, but it's not entirely permanent, it could come back and trigger everything."

Page 115

Conversion

Lois started to cry. "I just want my wonderful son back."

Mark walked into the room, "Hi Mom. Hi Dad."

Lois was stunned, "Your voice, it's deeper."

Dr. Murphy smiled, "We gave him some testosterone to trigger puberty, he should become a fine young MAN very soon now. Just remember, you have to take lithium every night, before bed. You'll be able to sleep at night and be awake during the day. If you stop, everything will get mixed up."

Homecoming

It had been such a long summer. To Mark it seemed like years, perhaps because so many of his years had been wiped from his memory. The last two years were like a dream, a fog. He could remember classes, lessons, but no friends.

Mark walked into the house and looked around. It seemed like a distant memory. He walked into the kitchen, it was difficult to remember. He remembered his mother cooking, but there was something else, he couldn't quite remember.

Lori and Linda ran down the stairs. Lori was wearing a skirt and sweater, she had just come home from school. She came over and gave Mark a hug. She stepped back, "What do you think of my skirt? I got it for school!"

Mark felt queasy, "It's nice. Excuse me." He ran into the bathroom. He was feeling sick, but not heaving. He washed his face and came back out.

Linda came down and hugged his waist. "Hi Markie, welcome home! Did you want to play dollies with me?"

Mark snapped. "Dollies are for GIRLS!" He almost spit it out.

Linda pulled away and ran back upstairs crying. Lloyd let out a chuckle.

Lois huffed at him. She went to the kitchen, "Hey Mark, did you want to help me cook?"

Mark sneered, "Cooking is WOMEN'S work."

Lloyd laughed, "That's my boy, let's watch the game.
The Corn Huskers are playing the CU Buffaloes."

Conversion

Mark nodded, "Oh, football, OK Dad." He went out to the living room and plopped on the couch. There was no enthusiasm, but his eyes were staring at the screen.

An hour later, Steve walked in. He walked into the living room and stopped when he saw Mark. "Hey runt, why are you in here? You're watching football?"

Lloyd barked, "Steve, sit down and shut up. Watch the game."

Steve was contrite. "Fine, this is just weird."

As they watched the game, Steve and Lloyd cheered the 'Huskers. Mark just watched the game. Even when they scored, Mark's cheer came about 5 seconds too late. It was like he didn't even know what he was watching.

When Lois came in and announced dinner was ready, Mark just got up and sat down. Lois asked, "Aren't you going to set the table?"

Mark sneered, "That's WOMEN'S work!"

Lois had the girls help her set the table, and Mark didn't move a muscle to help. When the food was brought out, Mark had a huge slice of roast beef, and a big glop of potatoes. He didn't even take a serving of the vegetables. Lois was puzzled, "Mark, don't you want vegetables?"

Mark shook his head. "No, I'm just a meat and potatoes guy!"

Even Lloyd was beginning to wonder if the hospital had gone too far. Mark was rude.

When dinner was finished, Lois asked Mark to help clear the table. Mark refused, "That's WOMEN'S Work! I won't do it."

Conversion

Then he went back into the living room to watch football. Lloyd joined him, along with Steve. The 'Huskers' won, but he didn't seem to care. He cheered, but it was obvious that he didn't even know this was his father's and Steve's favorite team. A few times he even cheered the wrong team but stopped when he realized that Lloyd and Steve weren't cheering. Mark went up to bed.

That night, Lois turned to Lloyd. "I really hate this New Improved Mark. He has been rude, and sexist, a bit too much like Steve. I want my old Mark back. I'd rather have my sweet boy in a dress, than this sexist little shit that won't lift a finger to help."

Lloyd hushed her. "Don't EVER let him hear you say that. You know what will happen if Marcia comes back, don't you?" He rolled his eyes into the back of his head and stuck his tongue out.

Lois shook her head, "No, I'd never let that happen. I'm not going to let them turn Mark into a vegetable. Never. If you approve it, I would leave you and take the kids."

Lloyd propped himself up. "Honey, you KNOW the alternative. If Marcia comes back, he will kill himself."

Lois shook her head. "NO! She said if she couldn't live as Marcia, she would kill herself. There is another option."

Lloyd fell back on the pillow. "It doesn't work that way. Boys can't be girls."

Mark spent a week getting used to being home. He was a rude sexist jerk the whole time. He refused to do anything he thought was "WOMEN'S WORK".

Lois knew that it was that stupid programming, but she hated the changes in her son. She so wanted to tell him about Marcia, but she didn't want to lose her son.

Conversion

On Saturday, Mark went outside. Lily came out and waved, "Hey Marcia, come on over."

At first, Mark didn't even notice the strange girl.

"Mark, come on over, I've missed you."

Mark walked over to the strange girl. Almost immediately, his eyes dropped to her newly budding breasts. "Nice tits," and he winked.

Lily crossed her arms over her breasts. "You're a pig. I was wondering if you would come over and help me pick out an outfit, but now I'm not so sure."

Mark looked like he was about to throw up. "Pick out an outfit, why the hell would I want to do a thing like that?"

Lily's eyes widened, "I don't know where you've been or what you've been doing, but I don't care. Just - - Never Mind!" and she ran back into the house.

Mark struggled for a minute. He tried to remember who this pretty girl was, why she was so nice to him, he knew her, but he couldn't remember what they did together or why they were friends.

Lloyd and Steve came out. "Mark, I'm taking Steve to soccer practice, did you want to come?"

Mark nodded. "OK. I'll come."

When they got to the field, Mark watched Steve's team practice. He realized that when Steve's team went to one end of the field, his father was happy, when it went the other way, his father was mad. When the practice was over, Steve's team won, and Mark saw that his dad was happy, so he smiled.

Conversion

Just then, the junior coach came over. "Hey Lloyd, Steve, did Mark come to play today?"

Lloyd shook his head. "I don't think so, remember last time?"

"Yeah, sorry about that, I should have been watching more closely. It won't happen again."

Mark was almost in a trance, "I want to play soccer."

Lloyd shook his head in disbelief. "Are you sure, Mark?"

Mark nodded. "I think so. Boys play soccer. I must play soccer." Without thinking he just walked out onto the field.

Within seconds, he was tripped and fell. A boy kicked him going after the ball. Mark curled up into a ball.

Suddenly he had a flashback. He saw the boys kicking him, but this time, the boys stayed in their zones, and there was no one near him. He kept waiting for the kicks, screaming in terror. The coach blew the whistle, and the boys stopped playing. Mark was still curled up on the green, sobbing.

Lloyd helped him up. "Mark, it's OK, nobody is hurting you. You're safe."

The coach fumed, "Forget it, I don't care if he is Steve's brother, I don't want to ever see him again! Especially not on my field! Get that FREAK out of here!"

Mark walked back to the car with Lloyd. When they got into the car, Steve was laughing. "Mark, you are such as Sissy Fairy."

Mark just smiled, but it was not a pleasant smile.

Conversion

When they got home, Lloyd and Steve went to watch football, but Mark just went upstairs to his room. He started reading a book, but his heart wasn't in it.

Mark came back to the kitchen. He whispered, "Mom, I'm so sorry I was so rude this week. If you want me to help in the kitchen, I can do it."

Lois smiled and hugged her son. "Oh, Mark, it's so great to have you back. Could you peel some potatoes?

Mark started peeling the potatoes. Lori came in, and the two of them finished peeling them.

He came over and smelled the chicken. "Smells good. Needs some lemon juice and soy sauce."

Lois smiled. "Great Idea, I'll try it. You always were a great cook!"

Mark smiled. "I think I still am."

Lois smiled and hugged him. "Welcome back, don't let anybody know."

Mark looked a little confused. "Thanks Mom."

After dinner, Mark gathered the laundry and took it downstairs. He started sorting the clothes. Lois walked in on him. She started to panic. "Mark, you can't do that anymore. Don't you remember why you did Laundry?"

Mark nodded, "I remember Mom. I remember everything"

Lois hushed him. "You can't tell anybody. You don't want to go back to that horrible place, do you? It might be even worse."

Conversion

Mark sneered. "Of course, I won't tell anyone, I'm never going back there, don't try to make me either. I don't trust you anymore. But I don't have to be a jerk and you need help with the housework, and I know how to do it."

Back to School

Mark returned to school. He couldn't fight the programming.
When he got too close to the girls, he got violently ill, but he had no
desire to be around the boys, even though he thought they were
cute.

He was still awful at sports, and gym, but there was no
overwhelming desire to get better either. Then he had to take a
shower with the other boys.

The boys started taunting him again. "Hey Marcia, stop flashing
your clit."

Another boy laughed "Yeah MARCIA, maybe you should go shower
with the GIRLS."

One of the boys pulled his sister's red bra out of his backpack "Here
Marcia, we'll put it on for you."

Mark began getting violently ill. He couldn't move. He was frozen
in place, and wanted to throw up, but he couldn't.

Two of the bigger boys grabbed the matching panties, "Here
Marcia, we'll put them on for you."

They grabbed his arms and forced him into the bra. Mark started
the dry heaves. He wanted to vomit but he couldn't, and he
couldn't stop heaving. The boys started to back away.

Mark kept heaving, wearing nothing but the bra and panties. He
couldn't stop retching long enough to get them off. His mind was
at war. He wanted to wear the bra, but the programming was
making him violently ill.

The coach came in and saw Mark, on the floor, trying to vomit,
heaving, and the red bra. Mark was curled up on the floor, just

sobbing and retching. The coach just stood there and watched. "Get up boy, get those ridiculous things off."

Mark couldn't move. His mind fought to remember a time when he could wear a bra. He remembered Lily, and the other girls. He remembered dressing up with them, but he was still retching. Then he remembered the torture sessions, the movies, and the shocks. All the memories came flooding back. "I hate them, I hate them, I hate those horrible people."

The coach was worried now. Mark seemed to be having a crisis. "I'll call your parents."

Mark reached back and snapped open the bra. "No, I'm never going back there. I'm not going to let them win." The rage in his eyes, his voice, his words, came pouring out.

The coach backed off. "Fine, get dressed before the next class comes in."

Mark dressed quickly, and in rage, stuffed the bra and panties into the bottom of the backpack.

At lunch, Mark saw Lily and his former friends sitting together at their usual table. He remembered that he used to sit there too. He went over to the table.

"Hi Lily, I wanted to apologize for being so rude to you when I came back. I don't know what made me do that. It was terrible and rude. I'm so sorry, and I won't do it again."

Judy had been badly hurt. "Maybe you should go sit with the boys if you want to be a sexist pig."

Conversion

Mark was despondent. He walked away and found a little table in the corner, far away from the door and the food, and ate. Then he pulled a book out of his bag and started to read.

A teacher came up to his table, "If you're done eating, you have to leave. We can't have you just hanging around the lunch room by yourself."

Mark grabbed his backpack and shuffled out. He had been rejected by his friends, the boys had humiliated him, and he just wanted to be alone. He went and hid in a stairwell.

Mark remembered the treatments in the hospital. He wanted to tell somebody, but he had been told that if he did, they would do something worse. He was angry, he felt so helpless, he felt so alone. He just wanted to disappear. He remembered that day during evaluation, when he talked to those other kids about suicide. He began to think about it.

A couple of boys he didn't know walked in. They lit up a joint. "Hey kid, you want a toke?"

Mark was angry at his parents. They had put him in that horrible place. He wanted to lash out. "Yeah, give me a toke."

"Got any money?"

Mark knew that drugs weren't free, but he hadn't been all that hungry, so he had $2 left of his lunch money. He gave it to them.

Mark took a big deep toke and held his breath as long as he could. He could feel himself getting a little dizzy. Finally, he let it out. He felt calm, and light. "Thanks guys."

"Hey, that's cool, any time, you know where to find us. At least we know you won't rat us out."

Conversion

The bell rang and Mark got up and went to his next class.

In class, he kept smiling. He wasn't all that high, but he felt better. He wasn't so angry. He paid attention and did the writing assignment. He felt calm, relaxed, and focused.

The rest of the day went smoothly. He even did well in math class. Algebra was so much easier than memorizing all those tables and trying to do the calculations. He liked that the problems were more like real world problems too.

When he got home, Lois was still at work. Mark took his backpack to his room and started to do his homework. Then he saw the red bra. He decided to put it right at the top of his underwear drawer so his mother could find it. He remembered her signing the papers that sent him to that horrible place. He WANTED her to see the bra, to know that he had won.

He went back to his homework and was almost finished when Lori came up.

Even though they were only 18 months apart, they had been very close. Mark realized that he had been very cold to his sister, if not even mean. He went to her room.

"Lori, I'm sorry I've been so nasty to you. I don't know what's wrong with me."

Lori smiled. "It's OK Mark, mom told me that you would be different when you came back from that place. She cried for days when you first went. Mom and dad were fighting about it after they came to visit you."

Mark nodded. "It was a horrible place, and they did terrible things to me in there. I never want to go back there again."

Conversion

Lori could see the pain. "Did you want to talk about it?"

Mark shook his head. "They told me not to, or they would send me back. It was so terrible." He started to cry.

Lori gave him a hug. "Mark, it's OK, you're safe now, and you're not being a jerk. I'm on your side."

When Lois came home, Mark and Lori helped her get the meal ready. Mark cooked the sauce and Lori did the noodles. Lois chopped the salad, and Mark showed Linda how to make salad dressing with sour cream, milk, and some blue cheese.

When Lloyd saw Mark in the kitchen, he stopped short. "What are you doing in the kitchen Mark? Come and watch the game with me."

Mark shook his head. "I'm really not that interested Dad. You and Steve love football, so you should watch the game. I don't really like football much. I never have. I'll just hang out with mom, she needs the help."

Lloyd paused. Was this a relapse? "Fine, I guess. Since you've always enjoyed helping out in the kitchen, it won't do any harm."

When Lloyd went out and turned on the game, Lois saw Mark give her a wink. She realized that the helpful boy she had always known was back. It would be their secret.

After dinner, Mark helped clear the dishes, then went up and finished his homework. That night, he locked the bedroom door, and put on the bra and panties. He retched, but he refused to allow that horrible place to win. He climbed under the covers and tried to relax. He thought about helping his mom in the kitchen,

Conversion

about the happy times with Lily, Sarah, Judy and his other girl friends.

It took almost an hour for the retching to stop, but when it finally stopped, Mark felt the soft satin, and began to relax. This was right, he was still a girl inside. They hadn't killed Marcia after all.

At lunch, he only had some chocolate milk and then went to the staircase and read. A few minutes later, the two boys were back and lit up. Mark walked over and gave them two bucks. He took a really big toke and held it as long as he could.

Marcia was furious that her parents had tried to kill her, and now she was rebelling.

One of the boys said "Hey, we're going to a drive-in movie this week-end. Weed and booze. Want to come?"

Mark smiled. "I'll let you know tomorrow."

The other boy said, "Just tell your parents you're going to a movie, they don't need to know WHERE you are watching the movie."

Mark smiled. "OK, that will work. Did you want to pick me up?"

The first boy, Larry said "No, just meet us at the corner store on 8th and Main. We'll pick you up there. Bring five bucks for the gas and pot."

Mark nodded. "What about the movie admission?"

The other boy, Roger, laughed. "We just hide in the trunk while Larry and his girlfriend drive through. That way we get in for free."

Larry smiled. "My dad has an LTD, we can put a bunch of guys in there if we want."

Rebellion

On Saturday, Mark went to the corner store and met up with Roger and Larry. He gave Larry the five dollars. Larry's girlfriend, Peggy, was in the front seat, and another boy, Alan, was in the back with Roger.

They drove about a mile, and stopped on a quiet suburban street, then the three boys in the back seat climbed into the trunk. They drove to the drive-in theater, and had no trouble getting through. Once they were inside, the boys got into the back seat.

Then Alan pulled out a pint bottle of whiskey. "Here, take a swig."

Mark took a small sip. It burned, and he coughed. He tried to talk. "It burns."

Roger laughed, "Never had hard liquor before? You'll get used to it, then you'll like it."

Mark took another swig, the second one didn't burn so bad.

When it got dark, the movie started, and Larry lit a joint. He passed it to Peggy, who took a big toke, and a big slug of whiskey. Then she passed it back to Roger.

Roger toke a big toke, then passed it to Mark, and after taking a big toke, passed it to Alan. Soon the car was filled with pot fumes, and they had finished the whiskey. Then Alan pulled out beer and passed a can to each of them. Mark didn't like the taste of the beer all that much, but he didn't care. He just wanted to fit in, so he drank.

The movie was a spaghetti western with Clint Eastwood. They really weren't paying all that much attention. Peggy was in the

Conversion

front seat kissing Larry, while the boys in the back were drinking and smoking dope.

About half way through the movie, Alan moved to the front seat, and Peggy climbed into the back with the two boys. Mark realized that the two boys in the front were kissing.

Next thing Mark knew, Peggy had her hands down his pants. Mark had worn the panties and was terrified she'd say something. Instead she whispered in his ear "Cute panties, want to feel mine?", then she put his hand up her skirt.

Mark felt the panties, they were silky satin, and had lace on the leg openings. He caressed her gently, feeling the satin, and suddenly she said, "Right there, just rub that spot." Then she turned to kiss Roger who was groping her breasts.

She had her hand in Roger's pants too. Mark felt himself getting a little hard, but still not very big. Within a few minutes, Roger let out a grunt, then a groan, then he said, "Peggy, you're the best."

Peggy turned to Mark. "Keep rubbing that spot baby, I'm so close." She gave Mark a kiss and then she gave a little grunt. Then she pulled back. "That was great honey. What's wrong with your little guy?" Then she took a good look, "Hey kid, how old are you?"

Mark looked terrified, "I'm 14."

Peggy spotted the lie. "How old?"

Mark's head dropped. "I'm 13, I'm sorry I lied"

Peggy giggled and hugged him. "It's OK kid, you're cute and you follow directions. Is this too much for you?"

Conversion

Mark nodded. "I've never done this before, I've never even kissed a girl until tonight."

Peggy laughed, "A virgin! How sweet! At least I know why you haven't shot your load, you haven't even hit puberty yet have you?"

Mark shook his head. "I'm a late bloomer ma'am."

Peggy kissed him on the forehead. "It's OK kid, my step dad made me do him when I was 12. Fortunately, he lost interest when I was 16 and started dating boys. Still, you're cool."

They watched the movie a while longer, and she put Mark's hand back up her skirt, right over her mound. Mark began to caress it, "That's good kid, just keep it right there. About 15 minutes later, she moaned loudly, and pushed his hand away.

By the time Mark got home, his head had started to clear. He walked through the door quietly and went up the stairs. His mother was up and waiting for him. "Did you have a nice time?"

Mark nodded, much of the second movie was a blur to him. He could barely even remember what it was. "Yes, Mom."

Lois could smell the booze, "You've been drinking, haven't you?"

Mark shook his head.

Lois held his head "Don't lie to me. I'd rather know the truth."

Mark nodded, "Yes mam, I drank a little."

Lois smiled, "Go to bed. We have church tomorrow, and you have to sing."

Conversion

Mark went into his room, took off his panties, and put them in the drawer. It had been a close call. Thank goodness Peggy didn't say anything when she discovered them.

The next morning, Mark woke up with a hangover. His head hurt, his mouth felt like he was sucking on a dirty dish rag. He got up to brush his teeth and got dressed for church. He wore a suit with a white shirt and a red tie. He looked in the mirror. It just looked weird. His pretty full lips and high rosy cheeks clashed with the suit. His lips were as red as the tie.

He came down the stairs and his family were waiting. His father and brother were wearing similar suits, and his sisters were wearing pretty dresses with lace and satin. Lori was wearing pantyhose, and Linda was wearing white tights.

When they got into the car, Linda sat on Mark's lap. She was so cute. Lori sat in the middle, and Steve on the end. Mark couldn't take his eyes off Lori's legs. They looked so smooth and shiny. He wanted to touch them, to feel them. Then he realized he wanted to wear them.

He turned to Linda and told her a story from the Bible, the story of Joseph and his brothers. Linda giggled as Mark started rattling off dozens of colors. Finally, he moved on to the part about the brother's jealousy, being sold and taken to Egypt, and telling the prophesy for Pharaoh. He finished the story just as they got to church.

When they got to Sunday School, Pastor Tom was there to talk to the Sunday School class. Mark and Steve were with the youth group. He saw Peggy sitting further down the row.

Pastor Tom spoke, "I came to talk to you about sins of the flesh. The good book says, 'Thou shalt not put unclean things into the body because the body is the Lord's temple'."

Conversion

He looked at Mark, then at Peggy, "Some people drink, or smoke, or do drugs, but this is the road to temptation and sin."

Mark just zoned out. He was sick of hearing Pastor Tom spew his judgmental opinions, throwing together various verses from all over the Bible to make some point, or to get a bigger collection. If it weren't for the youth group and the choir, he probably wouldn't want to go to church at all. He knew the Bible and knew the entire chapters from which Pastor Tom was pulling his selected verses. Clearly Pastor Tom has missed the bigger picture, the thinking behind the chapter containing the verse, and the book containing the chapter, and the chapters before and after the verse.

Mark just stared blankly at Pastor Tom. Fortunately, it was a short sermon and he went to prepare for the main service. Then they had a discussion on the preaching. Mark shared with his group the context of the teachings. He also quoted Jesus, "Jesus said that the unclean things are not what go into the mouth, but what comes out. Speaking hate, judgement, or falsely accusing someone so they will be punished, these are far filthier than shellfish or even wine."

The Youth Pastor was dumbfounded. He realized that Mark had not only turned Pastor Tom's pitch into hate speech, but he had made a dozen superior theological points. If Mark weren't so defiant, he might make a great preacher someday.

After class, Mark went to the choir room to get his robe and music. It was a song he knew well and was excited to sing it. He didn't have to do a solo, but he would be singing harmony with the other girls, altos, in the choir.

During rehearsal, his voice cracked three times. It was strange, like he couldn't control the pitch. He was visibly upset. They ran the

song a second time, and he cracked one more time. It was like a toad. The girls giggled at him.

He made it through the Anthem, but during the hymn, his voice started cracking again. He couldn't seem to control it.

After church, he came to his mom. "Mom, there's something wrong with my voice, I can't seem to sing right."

Lois pulled him into the living room. "Lloyd, it's time to give Mark the birds and bees talk."

Lloyd took Mark into his den. Mark sat on the couch, and his father sat next to him. Mark had a feeling of dread.

Lloyd started. "Son, your body is finally changing. Soon your penis will get larger, your testicles will drop, your voice will get deeper, you'll start growing a beard, and you'll get hair on your arms and legs. You might even get hair on your chest and your back."

Lloyd went on. "The girls your age are also going through changes. They will start growing breasts, they will get curves, and they will become beautiful women, like your mother."

Mark was about to cry, "Why daddy? Why do I turn into a man?"

Lloyd smiled, "Your testicles make testosterone, and that turns you into a man. Your testicles were inside you when you were born, but soon they will be coming down, and you will have a deep voice and become a man, like Steve, me, and your grandfathers."

Mark looked so sad, "OK, so I can't stop it?"

Lloyd smiled. "No, every little boy grows up to be a man, and you will be a man very soon."

Conversion

Mark looked at his hands, "Thank you dad, I understand."

Mark ran straight up to his room and cried for the rest of the afternoon. He didn't want to be a man. He wanted to be a girl. He wanted breasts. He was so angry he put the red bra and panties right at the front of his underwear drawer. He WANTED his mother to find them. Maybe she could help him become a girl.

Mark got up and did the laundry, he folded the clothes, and ironed the shirts and skirts, but he deliberately didn't put them away. He would make sure that his mother did it.

After dinner, he went for a walk. He walked around the park. He sat on a bench and listened to the traffic and looked up into the stars. The night sky was filled with stars, a beautiful night to just relax and enjoy the night.

When he came home, he went upstairs. The bra and panties were gone. He was certain that his mom had found them and would want to talk about them soon. Would she be coming up now that he was home? Would she talk to him tomorrow? Marcia could barely wait!

Nothing happened. Nothing happened that night. Nothing happened the next day. Nothing happened all week. Lois hadn't said a word to him. She hadn't even acknowledged that she had put away the clothes.

On Thursday night, Mark was taking a bath, and he felt something strange. It hurt, like someone punched him in the stomach. He pressed on his belly, down low. Suddenly he felt a pain that made him want to pass out. He looked down and saw a bulge between his legs. He realized it must be his testicle. He tried to push it back up inside. He started to cry. "No, no, no, no, NO, this can't be happening." A few minutes later, he had a pain on the other side. He looked down, and there were two bulges, two testicles.

Conversion

Mark was frantic. He tried pushing them both back up where they came from. It hurt so bad, when he tried to push them too far, but no matter what he did, they wouldn't stay put. He tried to squeeze them, but it hurt too much. He started to cry.

Finally, he had to get out of the tub and go to bed. He was so depressed. He wanted to sleep forever. How could he stop from being a man? He wanted to be a woman, with breasts, and he was going to become a hairy roaring beast instead. He wanted desperately to talk to someone, but he didn't want to go back to that horrible place.

He laid in his bed for hours, but he couldn't sleep. He couldn't sleep for several days. He snapped at people, was irritated easily, and wanted to be left alone.

A few days later, he was exhausted. He was falling asleep in class, he was not talking to anyone, he wasn't raising his hand. He didn't even talk to his mom. He stopped helping around the house, he just went up to his room. Often, he would come home from school and just fall asleep.

When Lois called up to Mark for dinner, he didn't respond. She went upstairs to wake him up.

"Mark, I won't make you help if you don't want, but you can't just ignore me when it's time for dinner."

Mark was defiant. "Did you put my underwear away?"

Lois nodded slowly, "You can't do that anymore Mark. Something terrible will happen. There are worse things than that place."

Mark snapped, "Something terrible IS happening Mother, my balls just dropped, and I'm on a one-way trip to becoming a hairy ugly

beast. My voice is starting to break. I can't do that Mom! I won't do it!"

Lois started to panic, "You can't talk that way. They would destroy your mind, you would be a vegetable. But they might do terrible things to you before that."

Mark fumed, "Like giving me shocks to my brain? Like torturing me for hours at a time? Like not letting me sleep for days at a time? Like making me want to throw up every time I saw a woman in a cute skirt? Like forcing me to like football, soccer, and boy stuff? Like making me hate to do anything associated with WOMEN'S Work?"

Lois's jaw dropped, her eyes widened. The panic was obvious.

"Yes Mom, I remember EVERYTHING. I remember you SIGNING the papers that put me in that horrible place. You agreeing to have me tortured, shocked, and brainwashed. Yes, I remember it ALL, Mom."

Lois started to cry. "I had no idea what they were doing. They said they were going to CURE you, that you wouldn't remember, that you would come out acting like any other typical boy."

Mark raged on, "They didn't CURE me mom, they made me WORSE. I can't sleep for a week, and then I can't do anything BUT sleep. Sometimes it feels like my mind is going a thousand miles an hour, other days, all I can think about is falling asleep. I DID act like a typical boy. I acted like a total jerk. I drove away all my friends, but I'm NOT like the other boys, and they all hate me too. I was FORCED to wear that bra and panties that you found in the drawer. I retched for what seemed like hours. I WANTED to wear it, but I got violently ill. I had to wear it half the night before I stopped wanting to retch."

Conversion

Lois panicked. "Mark, you're a boy, you have to accept it."

Mark growled, "I'm a boy and I hate it. Worse, I'm starting puberty. I wanted breasts and a big butt, and to be able to hang out with Lily and my other friends. ALL my friends are GIRLS! Instead you sent me to HELL for 90 days, and now I'm all alone and about to turn into everything I never wanted to be. And NOW, you DON'T want to TALK ABOUT IT!"

Lois started to sob. "I'm so sorry, I'm so sorry, I never meant for you to suffer, I never wanted them to hurt you. I wanted you to be HAPPY, I wanted you to be normal, like Steve. I love you, I was trying to help you."

Mark went cold. "I promise not to kill myself, because if I don't promise, you'll send me away again. If you don't want to talk to me about being a girl, then don't bother talking to me again. I'm not hungry, I'm not going to eat. Now GO AWAY!"

Lois walked away sobbing. For 13 years, Mark had been a wonderful, polite, sweet boy, even if he was a bit feminine. She had betrayed him, and now all she could hear was hate. Would Mark ever forgive her?

The next day at school, Mark went to the stairway. Larry and Roger shared a joint with him. They invited him to a party that Friday. They would meet at the same corner.

Mark didn't even ask for permission. After dinner, he walked out of the house, and went to the corner. The car picked him up, and they went to the party.

The party was at a house in the suburbs, no parents, a dozen kids, mostly Seniors, smoking, drinking, and popping pills. Roger offered him a joint and a drink, a glass of vodka and orange juice. Then he

Conversion

offered him a pill, a "downer". Mark washed the pill down with the drink.

Mark started feeling dizzy. Then a blonde girl came over and gave him a kiss. "Why don't we go to the coat room."

When they got inside, she shut the door. She gave Mark a kiss, then sat on the couch. Mark was feeling relaxed, happy, mellow. He sat down next do her and gave her another kiss. She put his hand up her skirt. He felt the silky panties and found the little mound. She told him what to touch.

After a few minutes, she pushed him onto the floor, and said "Eat me". Mark knew it was probably the drugs, but he couldn't resist. He did what she wanted, and soon she was done. She stood up and said, "Don't move".

A minute later, a young man came in, dropped his pants, and told Mark to "suck it."

Mark looked at the young man. He was handsome, trim. Mark imagined himself as a girl and did what he was asked. For the next hour or so, he serviced one guy after another, then a few girls.

As Mark's head began to clear, he tried to stand up. He was dizzy but walked out of the coat room. Alan came over and offered him another drink. It was a rum and coke, but it was bitter. It didn't take long for the powder to take effect. Alan walked Mark back into the coat room and had him kneel next to the couch. Mark serviced nearly every guest at the party. By the time he got home his jaw was sore. It was after 2AM.

He didn't even try to creep in. He walked through the door, walked up the stairs, and walked into the bathroom. He gargled with mouthwash. Then he sat to pee and flushed the toilet.

Conversion

He got undressed and climbed into bed. He turned on the light and started to read.

Lois walked into his room. "Where have you been?"

Mark sneered, "A party."

Lois could smell the booze and the pot. "Have you been drinking?"

Mark was cold. "Yeah, and smoking pot, and popping pills"

Lois fretted. "You could have been hurt, or raped, or worse!"

Mark smiled. "Well I did give a bunch of head and blow jobs."

Lois said, "You're going to church tomorrow."

Mark smirked. "Can I wear a dress?"

Lois smiled. "Don't be silly."

Mark went stone faced, "Then I'm not going."

Lois glared. "Do I need to pull your father in here?"

Mark snarled, "So he can give me 40 lashes with the belt? Another trip to the hospital? A lobotomy?"

Lois softened, "I know you're mad, but you need to face reality, you are a boy and you can't become a girl."

Mark went cold, "Fine, and I won't kill myself, but I'm not going to church to listen to that self-righteous Pastor Tom. Did you know that he groped me in his office?"

Lois shook her head. "You're lying, he would never do that."

Conversion

Mark nodded. "You see, that's the problem. If he did, and you're calling me a liar, then you've just betrayed me again. If he didn't and I'm lying, you have no way to check it out."

Lois panicked, "You're lying"

Mark was furious. "I also got groped at IdRaHaJe!"

Lois started crying. "You're LYING!"

Mark's eyes narrowed, he was seething with hate. "And your precious hospital, that you signed me into for 90 days, they tortured me by putting a metal dildo up my ass and a wire down my dick and giving me long painful shocks while I was strapped to a chair watching pornography. They raped me every day for hours at a time, while I watched in terror as women took their clothes off, put them on, kissed boys, kissed girls, while boys kissed boys. And they gave me drugs that made me want to throw up. THAT'S what YOU did to me MOM!"

Lloyd heard the shouting and walked in. "What's going on here? Why are you yelling at your mother?"

Lois shook her head. "Nothing dear, go back to bed."

She came to sit on Mark's bed. "I'm sorry baby, you don't have to go to church if you don't want. I understand. You've already been through hell. I won't do that to you again."

Mark spent the next few months living a triple life. He only partied on weekends, turned in excellent schoolwork, and went to church, even though he couldn't sing anymore. This was a concession to his mother, with the understanding that he was not to be left alone with ANY pastor, especially Pastor Tom.

Conversion

Mark saved up money and began buying his own wardrobe. He had panties, a nightie, slips, a skirt, a bra, and a blouse. He even managed to buy a wig at a thrift shop.

The parties were getting strange. He couldn't remember them. Sometimes, he didn't even remember coming home. His mouth and jaw were sore, but no memories.

He decided to go to the party dressed as a girl. He got dressed, did his makeup, and went to the corner. When the car pulled up, he used his best girl voice, "Mark couldn't make it, may I come instead?"

The boys were eager to have the cute girl in the car. It was only after he had been in the car several minutes that they realized it was Mark, not Marcia.

Alan smiled. "Dude, you are one HOT babe. Give me a kiss."

Mark leaned over and gave him a gentle kiss. Alan pulled him in with both arms and gave her a passionate romantic kiss. Marcia responded, she liked it. She wanted more.

When they got to the party, Alan gave her a drink. It was a sweet drink, it burned, and she quickly chugged it. Then Alan led her into the coat room. She kissed him passionately. Then Alan dropped his pants and said, "On your knees, slut".

As Marcia was pleasing him, he was groaning with pleasure. "We made OK money on Mark, but we can make five times more with you Marcia."

It triggered memories. She remembered how many boys and girls he had pleasured. She remembered being led into the room and pleasuring people for hours. Fat ones, skinny ones, ugly ones, pretty ones, and smelly ones. They had been SELLING her.

Conversion

Marcia stopped, and looked up with a smile. "OK, but I want a cut."

Alan smiled. "Fine, you get 20%, and drugs."

Marcia sneered. "Doesn't seem fair, since I'm doing all the hard work."

Alan scoffed. "Come on, you like it! You've been doing it for free up to now! Besides, there are expenses. The house, the booze, getting the right guests, and keeping the cops away."

Marcia smiled. "25%, You still get to split the lion's share. Better than nothing. That's my price for Marcia."

Alan acted like she had twisted his arm; it was less than he was paying the other girls, but Marcia wasn't a girl. "Fine, it's a deal."

Alan got her another drink, she knew she was blacking out, but she didn't care. At the end of the night, Alan gave her a hundred dollars. She was tired, her knees were sore. They dropped her off at the corner, and she went home. She got undressed and went to sleep.

The next day, after church, he walked to the mall, and got some lovely new clothes. He hid them well. He bought a board for the bottom of his drawer and put a hole in it.

For months, Marcia went to the parties, earning money so she could buy clothes. Her outfits got much sexier and sluttier. But she had to hide them carefully. There were false bottoms in all her drawers, and a false floor in the closet.

Mark was still having trouble sleeping for days, even weeks at a time, then got so tired she could barely stay awake.

Conversion

At one of the parties, Marcia got mouthy with one of the guys at the party, implying that he was tiny, that he was premature, and that he was a lousy lover, right in front of his girlfriend who had just called her a whore.

The guy beat her up, but not too badly. Alan and Roger came to her rescue. After that, she stopped being invited to the parties.

Mark started drinking on his own. He couldn't get booze, but he could go to the grocery store and get mouthwash, cold medicine, Benadryl, and sleeping pills.

Lois finally decided to take Mark to a psychiatrist. She promised Mark that he would not be hospitalized or held for observation.

Initially, the doctor decided the problem was anxiety. He put Mark on Valium. The company that made Valium was paying a bonus for each new patient, and the doctor figured he could make a few bucks while he was helping the boy.

Mark was also taken to a therapist. He knew he couldn't talk about Marcia, so he talked about getting beat up, the nightmares, and staying awake all night and sleeping all day. Each visit, he just seemed terribly tired, like he had given up.

Finally, the doctor switched him over to Lithium, and things improved. Mark was sleeping through the night, alert during the day, and getting better.

One day, he finally decided he would try talking to his therapist about Marcia. The therapist told him he was suffering from Gender Identity Disorder, and that he should stop dressing, and face the reality that he was becoming a man.

Conversion

One day, at church, the choir director came up to him after the service. "I've heard you singing the hymns. I want you to sing in the adult choir. Can we see what kind of range you have?"

As the director played the arpeggios, he kept going lower and lower. Mark's voice was strong, his pitch nearly perfect, and his range was nearly 3 octaves. The director was delighted, "Mark, you have a beautiful bass voice, please sing bass for us."

Mark was ready to break down in tears. "I'll think about it."

Mark hadn't dressed for weeks. He came home from school early. He tried to get dressed, but nothing fit. He was too big. His feet were too big, his shoulders were broad, and his face had dark stubble and he had gotten taller. He looked at his reflection in the mirror and was disgusted. The pretty girl was gone. What was left was obviously a guy in a dress. He looked hideous and nothing he could do would change that.

He put the clothes away in his secret compartments. He prayed for all he was worth that God would please turn him into a girl. He prayed that God would take away those testicles. But in his heart, he knew it was too late. This body would never be a pretty girl again.

In Social Studies, he had learned that the Hindus and Buddhists believed in reincarnation, that after you die, you just get reborn into a new body. He realized that Jesus promised eternal life, yet people kept on dying. Could it be that there was the option of Heaven, Hell, or reincarnation? Maybe when this life ended, he could come back as a girl?

But what kind of girl would he be? A girl in Nebraska? A girl in a big city? A white girl? A black girl? A girl in Saudi Arabia, one of many wives? A girl in Africa, where they do clitoridectomies? A girl

Conversion

in China, where women are little more than slaves? Maybe living a better life would lead to a better next life?

For months, Mark was the ideal boy. He was nice, polite, he sang in the choir, he did good deeds anonymously. Meanwhile, he planned his termination. He had lost all his friends, he had been rejected by the boys. He was alone. He hated this man's husk.

Hi doctor had warned him not to drink on his new medication. What would happen? He went to the library to look it up. It turns out that Lithium changes your liver so that it can't process alcohol. Instead of urine, it would become formaldehyde. Death would be quick and relatively painless, like falling asleep.

For the next two weeks, he doubled his dose. Building up a concentration. He had no trouble convincing Roger to sell him a pint of brandy. He bought a pretty dress, panties, and a bra, in his new size. Perhaps, if he wore a dress when he died, he could be a girl in whatever came next.

At church, he agreed to be baptized, much to the joy of Pastor Tom. Mark thought it so ironic, the Pastor had no idea that the baptism was to prepare him for death.

That night, Mark dressed himself in his new outfit, then drank the entire pint. Then he laid down in the bed. Within minutes, he was sleeping. Never to wake again. The breathing slowed, then stopped.

By the time they discovered he was gone, it was too late. His father stripped him naked and put him in jockey shorts. The police found his stash and agreed to keep the details out of the papers.

At the funeral, there were almost 300 people. Steve's friends, Lloyd's family and coworkers, Lois's coworkers, people from the

church. Pastor Tom said very little about Mark, and nothing about Marcia. He spoke well of the family.

Lily was there, mourning the loss of a girl she once loved. A girl named Marcia.

Printed in Great Britain
by Amazon

78801703R00088